Life Supports

K.G. WATSON

ISBN: 978-1-989506-17-2
Cover Design: Alex Goubar
Cover Photo: Mae Watson

www.pandamoniumpublishing.com
pandapublishing8@gmail.com

DEDICATION

To my wife, Mae,
who keeps me connected to this world
and welcomes me back from the others
into which writing takes me

CONTENTS

www.pandamoniumpublishing.com

A boutique publishing house located in Hamiltion, Ontario, Canada.

Pandapublishing8@gmail.com

1
THE EPISODE

BEEP…BEEP…BEEP…the irritating sound pushed in upon me as I struggled back to awareness.
BEEP…BEEP…BEEP…the damn noise wouldn't stop. Where is that sound coming from? I opened my eyes into a glare that made me close them again.
BEEP…BEEP…BEEP…chirped the annoying signal.

"That's not my alarm," I thought. I rolled onto my side to punch at whatever was now calling frantically. I couldn't get my hand out of the blankets.

I squinted against the glare. I could see the blurry face of my daughter hovering too close and beside her appeared another in some sort of green uniform.

"Dad," said my child looking up from her phone screen, eyebrows arched. "You're awake."

"Mr. Scottman," said the other face. "Glad to see you're awake now."

"Would you turn off that God damned beeper?" I asked. I struggled to get my arm out from under the bedding as I looked at the machine that continued its hysterical piping.

"I can't understand you," said the face. "Oh. Let me turn down the heart monitor."

The shrill alarm stopped, and I closed my eyes in relief. I sighed and looked around for my glasses.

"Dad," said my daughter, "You've …

"What are you doing here?" I asked in confusion. I looked for my bedside alarm clock, the lamp, the laundry basket with yesterday's clothes. None of those things was in sight - just a blank wall. Even the room was the wrong colour.

"Where am I?" I demanded.

"Dad," my daughter persisted, "You've had a stroke. I can't understand what you're saying. Please stop trying to move. We'll get you whatever you need. You're in the hospital now and you've just awoken."

"What the hell are you talking about?" I demanded. "What am I doing here? I'm not sick." I looked angrily about the room. "Where are my clothes? I got my other arm free and yanked at the bedsheet, "Get me out of here."

"Mr. Scottman," said the other person. "Be still. You'll hurt yourself." She pushed down on my arm.

"Dad," commanded my daughter, like a drill sergeant. "Be still. Stop moving."

I was shocked. I never remember hearing that tone from her. I slumped into a sideways heap. Hands pushed me back under covers.

"What the hell is going on?" I asked. And then felt unspeakably weary - like the air had just fizzled out of my balloon. *God I'm tired,* I thought. *I'll just rest a moment.*

I guess I must have dozed off. When I woke up, I looked sideways through a dim space at a fuzzy palisade of white bars just beyond my nose. It took me a moment to recognize them as steel bars that separated me from the white wall I'd seen before. I tried to reach out and touch them with the hand right beside them, but I couldn't do it. I swung my right arm across to touch the verticals. Cold and smooth and hard. *Yep, steel,* I thought, *but why were they there?*

I looked the other way. Another line of metal stakes stood guard. Beyond was a wall of blinking lights and dancing digits. A bright line snaked up and down but never seemed to go anywhere. It left a florescent trail that faded behind it. A pole stood in front of the display with white tendrils hanging down. Drops inside a capsule on the tube caught a light and winked on and off as they formed and fell. It made me think of a metronome - the one on the organ at home. *Quarter note is 128*, I calculated.

... so easy to let the hymns drag, I thought and wondered why that thought came up. *I don't have a service till Sunday. Wait. Don't I have a funeral on Friday? Yes. Mr. Gallagette died. I'm dredging up all the moldy oldies the family thought was appropriate. Right. I was doing that when ... the phone rang.*

There were moans and wails in the distance.

"What's wrong with that person?" I asked the room. And then the effort of trying to lift myself up and call to anyone overwhelmed me. *Jeez, I'm tired,* I thought.

"You've shown good improvement," declared the sanctimonious youngster in the white coat and clipboard.

I glared at him with all the incredulity I could muster.

"What the hell would you know about it?" I growled. My daughter sitting at my bedside laid a hand on my arm.

"I see you are eating yourself, toileting yourself. Your meds are in order. You're good to go," he declared with a dismissive scrawl across his page.

I raised my head and was drawing breath. My daughter patted my arm, then gripped it. I sighed and looked down.

"Have you seen the pureed stuff they serve us here?" I muttered. It brought another quiet rebuke from my daughter's hand.

"Yes, Mr. Scottman," the doctor continued blithely. "I didn't get that, but I have ordered physio on that arm and for your speech. You're not going home just yet. A little more healing to happen there. Your family was lucky to get you a bed at the Evercare Retirement Home. They have a good program of rehab that we've worked with before; you'll be in good hands. I'll sign you over to your GP for follow-up." He rustled another page to the top of his pile and scribbled something.

"So," he stuck out his hand and when I didn't put out mine, patted my arm, "you'll be moving out this afternoon. Glad to make your acquaintance. Keep going on your physio." He stood back and was on to the next page on his clipboard before he turned and headed out the door.

I tipped my head back onto my pillow and looked at the ceiling.

"He saved your life, Dad. He's one of the best in the world and he gave you mobility and clear thinking and the ability to look after yourself. I know how important that is to you. That's seven out of ten. That's incredible considering where you were when you came in. In the Retirement Home you won't have to prepare meals, just concentrate on getting the other faculties working.

"No meals to prepare, just eternal gruel," I said, "and the need to kill time," I added.

"Write it on the whiteboard," my daughter said as she handed it over.

I plucked the marker pen from the holder, grabbed the cap in my teeth to yank the pen free and blew the cap across the room. I drew a couple of steadying breaths. It wasn't fair to take out my rage on my daughter. I closed my eyes till I could breathe regularly again. *Fri - Funeral*, I wrote. The board slipped and the pen slid across the surface. I raised my hand, pen now held like a dagger to stab the board when Jean grabbed my hand and took the pen from me.

"Catharine looked after it. You had all the music pulled out for the service when you took your … spell. She'd been practicing all those pieces. You taught her well. She says she knew some of them already because they are regulars at her old church at home."

I nodded. The rattle of the lunch cart caused us both to look up. The person driving it swept a tray onto my bedside table. It was just as well the table was on my dead side; I glared at it and then the retreating back.

"Dad," Jean chided warningly. "You create a scene and they'll have you in irons and likely force feed you for dinner. That," and she pointed to the tepid slurry in the bowl, "is the way out of here. Think of yourself as Humphrey Bogart pulling the African Queen. You have to drag that boat through the swamp, leeches and all. But salvation is at the end."

I looked daggers at her, but she didn't flinch. I blinked first. I rolled across and grabbed the bowl by its rim as my daughter moved to pick up the spoon. In the time she took to move my glass of water and extricate the tool from the serviette, I had tipped the bowl down my throat, took three big slugs to clear the bowl and pulled it away. I heaved a sigh and pointed to the water glass.

Jean wiped the dribble at the corner of my mouth and handed me the tumbler.

"That wasn't bad now, was it." she declared.

"Actually, it wasn't half bad," I garbled but the noise only confused my daughter.

"I'll take that growl as a vote not to ever see it again," Jean interpreted.

I finished off the apple sauce in the second bowl with only a few drips onto the tray before a nurse came by. Jean bent to clean out the shaving gear, magazine, iPad and noise cancelling earphones from the shelf under the bedside table into a bag and left me with the clothes I'd arrived in.

"I see you have finished," the nurse complimented with a dazzling smile. "Your son is downstairs to take you to Evercare. Time to get you dressed," she said and then manhandled me into underwear, a freshly ironed, long-sleeved white shirt, V-neck sweater, and freshly ironed dress pants. Socks and slip-on shoes followed. "I know you can walk on your own and would prefer to do so," she continued, "but I'm under orders to take you in our limo." She pushed the wheelchair to the bedside. "Have you got your personal things?"

Jean held them up as I slid into the worn seat on wheels.

"Buckle up sir," the nurse said as she released the breaks on both sides. "Please remain seated until the coach comes to a complete stop." And off I went to a life I had not imagined in my worst nightmare, a week ago.

2
EVERCARE

"My Dad has taken a stroke, as I explained on the phone," Donald said to the Business Administrator at the Evercare Retirement Home. They were sitting in her office. Donald was still reeling from the shock of having to find accommodation for me. To see a sympathetic face opposite was an encouraging start to the meeting.

"Dad's 'event,'" as Donald described it happened only ten days ago. Donald could still not get used to calling it a stroke. Even as I lay comatose in the bed, the doctor could confidently say that I would not be returning home safely. I would be brought out of the induced coma the next day. It would be then that a more confident assessment could be made but no matter what, the doctor said, he could only keep me in hospital for a week at most, after I became conscious. The family needed to act speedily if they were going to be part of the accommodation solution. If they didn't, the hospital would discharge me to the first available suitable site. Donald and Jean had then blitzed several of the possible options and soon realized all the nursing homes were not the same.

"Your Dad will need months of physiotherapy to address the paralysis of his left arm and loss of my voice," the medical staff said.

Neither of my children could accommodate me in their small apartments. I needed the services and care a Nursing facility could provide but I wasn't an invalid. That was why the Doctor had suggested Evercare. The residents had a certain amount of independence or only needed special support and training to gain it. I seemed to fit those criteria. That all poured out in a rush and now Donald was waiting for some sort of response from the Administrator across the desk.

"We're pleased to have the doctor's recommendation. We have looked after patients of his in the past and found we work well together. Our staff here are well-trained also - stroke rehabilitation is a specialty of ours. Many have graduated from here back to their own homes when they regain the skills they need."

Donald was feeling optimistic. Maybe there was some light down this tunnel.

The Administrator suggested they tour the facility before they signed any paperwork. The dining facilities were elegant.

"Someone will even cut up your Dad's meat rather than serve food that had been processed through a blender as long as your Dad can cope," he was assured. Donald made the point that his Dad was a big meat and potato guy. The Administrator chuckled knowingly.

The rehab facility was spacious, airy, and ablaze with light reflecting from chrome equipment. Patients were being guided through routines by caring staff whose bright voices and cheering encouragement told Donald this was the right place for Dad. The small swimming pool and hot tub looked like icing on the cake.

They shook hands with the nurse in her suite of treatment rooms for the dentist, pediatrist, chiropractor and other rotating professionals.

"The library bus stops weekly. We have excursions and shopping at the big malls with our own bus," added the official as they passed the large sitting area.

God, I'd like to move in here, Donald thought as they followed the carpeted hallway to the room his Dad would occupy. The warm glow and confident hopes came to a crashing collapse as they stepped into the bedroom.

"Ohhhh," Donald moaned.

"I know it looks small," the Administrator said, "but we try to have our residents spend their waking times outside their rooms to keep their social skills honed." She closed the hall door to reveal a sliding door to a large walk-in closet behind it. "The closet is really quite roomy to take seasonal clothing on the lower level and off-season above." She waved into a space like a yard shed and then to the doorway to the washroom opposite. "The bathing and toilet facilities are large enough to accommodate wheelchairs," the Administrator commented.

Donald glanced in and agreed with the assessment. "No doubt it's big enough to swing a cat," he said.

"This part isn't clear to me," Donald said as they turned back to the bedroom. "This room holds the bed." It was squarely centered on the wall facing the door. "I can see a small desk and TV might sit there, and maybe a chair for a visitor over here," he pointed to narrow spaces flanking the bed.

"Yes," picked up the Administrator too quickly. "There is room for a narrow desk unit holding a computer monitor and keyboard. "If you have a favourite chair, it could be fitted in as long as it doesn't tilt back."

"I haven't made myself clear, I guess. My Dad is a Concert and Church organist," Donald announced. "He will come with his rehearsal organ. The Doctor said he'd probably be able to play with his right hand. Getting his left hand active might be part of his therapy, but there is no way he in coming without that organ."

"My son has an organ for the band he plays in," the Administrator said. It's a keyboard about…" and held her held his arms slightly out from her sides.

Donald slipped out his phone from a holster and spun through a photo gallery, then passed it to the Administrator.

"Ohhhh," breathed the administrator.

"Well we couldn't have that thing booming through the building," she said in alarm.

"Dad flips the switch and you can only hear it through earphones," Donald explained. "He will have to have it with him both as part of his therapy and mental well-being. It will have to be where the bed is, and maybe a cot would fit in that corner," Donald said pointing to the right.

Frost descended on the room.

"That would be quite out of the question," the Administrator replied. "We have regulations we must follow about access to a patient in bed. Such a large instrument could not be accommodated."

The interview that had reached the closing stage was slipping out of hand. There was no doubt that young Mr. Scottman would move Scottman senior in as soon as possible but the organ was an unexpected addition to the plan. The Administrator tried a bit of backpedaling.

"How big is the … unit?" she asked.

"Without the pedalboard, it is thirty-five inches from front to back. It will slide sideways through the door," Donald assessed.

The woman nodded.

"But on the floor, it needs six feet side to side." He pointed to the wall where the bed was. "I think it would take that whole wall with a small table beside for the music in use, or his four-drawer filing cabinet. The window light would make it a bright space to work in."

"When the pedalboard is in place, it will come out to here," Donald said stepping back from the headboard of the bed almost to the foot. "Would there be enough space to turn the bed sideways and tuck it along the closet room wall?"

"Well it would restrict access of staff to the bed. They must be able to get to both sides of the bed."

"Is a narrower bed available? How about putting it on wheels to slide out at bedtime and back tight against the wall in day? How about a Murphy bed that folds into the wall?"

Plainly, her client was trying to work out a solution and the Administrator took the cue to join in the process. But she still had to retain her position of control. Before she could dismiss the request, Donald jumped back in.

"I can see that every other room I looked into as we walked down the hall is set up just like this one. I can see that such a layout meets all your needs but I'm trying to solve a huge problem and we are within a whisker of doing it. We both need to think of the man who will be coming here. Is there room for him between the regulations? The doctor was effusive in his praise of your facility. Surely that counts for something."

Madame Administrator did not want to risk disappointing a significant practitioner who had sent them a lot of business.

"If he was to have a different sized bed, it leads to bedding and laundry problems and emergency evacuation rehearsals," the Administrator stated with authority.

The last point was a straw she threw out to buy time.

"Look," Donald said, "I don't want to get into a tit-for-tat argument. Everything we have agreed on looks like it can go ahead if we can just solve this bed issue. Dad has been sleeping on a camp cot at home because he didn't like the emptiness of the big bed after Mom died. With his organ, he can expect years of healthful living the doctors tell us. That could be a benefit to your establishment - the security of a long-term arrangement. Surely in this world, there is a small bed that would fit in here along with his organ. If his bed can only be one size and that is it," he gestured to the one in the room, "could he put the organ somewhere else and practice on it daily?"

The Administrator flared at the thought of having a patient take over communal spaces.

"That is not possible," she said dismissively. But the radical alternative gave her a chance to offer an olive branch. "I would need to confer with others. You realize there are many matters to consider here."

David caught the hint. *She doesn't want to do anything wrong. She needs permission from someone up her chain,* David thought. *If something goes wrong, it will be that person's fault.*

"Could you follow up on that and get back to me?" he asked.

They agreed to meet the next day. Donald got the doctor to call and offer a few more compliments. When Donald returned it was to accept grudging accommodation of a smaller bed that, with great difficulty, the establishment could provide.

"It could work out if we made appropriate changes," the Administrator summarized.

So, they pushed shadow pieces about for a while to reach an arrangement they thought would suit.

Having worked out a place for the organ, Donald quit while he was ahead. He didn't mention his father's collection of music.

Assessing the altered floor plan, the Administrator cautioned that there would be no room for guests to sit.

"If Dad is in bed, they can sit on the organ bench," Donald decided glancing back and forth as he imagined the layout. "If Dad is up, he'll be at the organ and guests can either stand beside him there, on sit on the bed. He can have guests, besides family, can't he?" Donald asked.

The Administrator looked up sharply.

"My Dad has students who have come for lessons. If they used earphones could they work here?" Donald was making this up. It had been years since he had pupils, but he asked anyway.

The Administrator nodded carefully. This was just the sort of creeping expansion she feared.

"He'd have to respect our other residents."

"You'll like my Dad," Donald assured her.

"Well let's return to my office and we can do the paperwork then if we're in agreement?" the Administrator invited.

3
THE REVEAL

As I settled into the car in the shotgun seat to leave the hospital, it was with relief. Yes, they were all nice people, but God I hate feeling like an invalid. The feeling of release and freedom lasted long enough to try to reach for my seatbelt.

"Shit," I spat out when I realized I couldn't catch the buckle of the seatbelt with my left hand and pull it across my chest to snap into the latch.

Donald immediately saw my distress and caught the meaning of the garbled sound I made. I pulled back so he could reach across, grab the buckle, pull out the strap and snap me in. Even so it was a wrestling match.

It was a quiet ride for a couple blocks. I think the kids were trying to decide how to tell me I wasn't going home and who got the short straw.

"We're taking you to the Retirement Home, Dad," Jean said from the back seat. "You need more physio on your voice and arm. We moved your dresser into your room, so you've got clothes. Steak is on the menu for tonight - little pieces of steak from miniature cows they keep."

I held up my right hand in a thumbs-up salute.

"What about the organ?" I asked but it came out as nonsense noise.

"The physiotherapists? Oh, they're killer cute," Donald replied.

I shook my head and sighed. I'd know soon enough.

When we pulled up in front of the Terminal Care Retirement Home, I managed to get my right hand over to undo the seatbelt latch. That was a bright spot in the day. Before letting it go, I tried following the buckle back to its retracted position and then pulling it out with my right hand and across my body to the latch again. It worked. I couldn't help but smile as I got out of the car.

As a group we paraded through the lobby and sitting area to the office of the high-priced help. She saw us coming through the window wall around her desk and came, smiling and power-suited, to greet us. I could feel her laser eyes looking deeply into mine before I glanced away. We went through the pleasantries and then the head honcho took me to where I'd be staying. It was down a long hallway, deep in carpet, muffled in sound.

As we walked, I looked into any room with an open door. Straight ahead was a bed where a shape lay framed in sheets, lit by the glow from a TV screen I could not see but which must have been around the corner just inside the doorway. My soul sank after the third copy.

Donald led us into my room, hitting the light switch as he passed. I looked down and gritted my teeth prepared for another hospital room.

There was a washroom on the left. I don't know what was behind the hall door that opened to cover the space to my right. It hung open as I came in. Between the walls of a short hall which in every other room had framed a bed with a body was … I had to blink to be sure it wasn't a mirage. The others were ahead and had turned the corner to be out of sight to my right.

I felt completely alone, like they had disappeared, and I was looking at heaven's gate. I realized I had taken two steps into the room and had stopped dead. I must have been there … I don't know how long - a second? A minute? When I shook my head and looked to my right, three faces were riveted, wide-eyed, on me. My mouth must have been open. I shook myself to shut my gaping mouth and looked back at it. It was my organ! The one I practice on a couple of hours a day! When I looked back at the faces they were smiling, and I realized I was laughing with tears running down my face.

I looked back at the center of my world for longer than I cared to admit. My slippers, the ones I change into when I'm working, were on the shelf at the left end of the keyboard. On the other end, two pencils lay, pointed sharply. The lamp stood ready to brighten any page on the stand.

Jean and Donald, I realized, were pretty teary-eyed as well. Rather than try to say anything, I held my hand over my heart and nodded gratefully.

I took the two next steps to the end of the bench and slid onto it. My feet slid onto the pedals as though magnets attracted them. I did a heel and toe up them silently, unconsciously. Daylight, but no sun, streamed in from a window to my right. It would nicely illuminate the music stand in daytime. But where was the music? I looked around to my children in unspoken question. Donald pointed to my left where one of my four-drawer filing cabinets stood. *It should be on the right,* I thought so I can reach it easily. But if it were, it would partly block the window. *Rightly placed,* I agreed.

On top of the filing cabinet I realized when I looked back, was my register, sitting atop a pile of its earlier brethren. My breath caught with relief. On those pages was the record of every day of practice, every concert, every service I had ever played on the organ.

My first teacher gave me the first time on my very first lesson. I couldn't reach the pedals when I started but I had been playing piano long enough then to know the keyboard. My lesson ended. While I was shaking with the thrill of the moment, he presented me with something that looked like a banker's ledger from a Victorian business. It must have weighed ten pounds.

The book was leather-bound and filled with a thousand numbered, unblemished, blue-lined pages. My teacher told me to write the date in the upper right side of the first page and handed me his fountain pen to do it.

Opposite on that line, on the left side of the page, he told me to write the address and city where we were. Underneath I was told to write the names of the pieces that had taken my time, the source book from which I worked and how long the session had been.

Near the left margin, under *Comments* he told me, "As you get better, you will write there what you did well and poorly, what you need to do to get better, how you feel from what you did."

I suddenly felt the weight of my lifetime bearing down on my skinny shoulders. *This was too much,* I thought.

"Suppose I want to quit?" I asked.

He slid the book over to read what I had written, then looked at me, "Think back a few minutes to how you felt when you stopped playing. Do you remember that shiver?"

I nodded.

He passed the book back to me, closed.

"I believe you will not quit - you cannot quit. You were born for this instrument. "This," and he patted the book, "will be the record of your life-long love affair with more than you can imagine. Now run along; I'll see you next week."

That moment, so long ago, flashed through my mind when I saw my journals stacked on top of the filing cabinet. I swung around on the bench to my audience of expectant faces. The tears were still trickling down my cheeks. I sniffed and turned abruptly to the keyboard. I flipped the switch on and before anyone could move, jammed my right hand down onto the four signature chords of Handel's masterpiece. My feet found the bass accompaniment without a glance.

"Hallelujah." It was thunderous.

The lady-in-charge jumped out of her skin. Horror swept over her; this is exactly the sort of disturbance she had feared. Shouts of amazement came from the hallway. Scottman spun on the bench and bowed appreciatively.

In the laughs and tears of the others, she had to agree that she had done the right thing, but she could sense problems coming.

With the cheering over, she led the group towards the dining room. Scottman had to fend off delighted greetings and responses from others in the hallway which only raised her anxiety another notch. He just nodded and smiled, held a hand over his heart like I was taking a curtain call. She left them to dine in a private room off the main dining room. She saw the kids leave; they had work to go to. She saw Mr. Scottman turn, shoulders sagging and start back to his room.

The walk down the hall threatened to press the buoyancy of the dinner into the carpet, but I knew I would be safe when I got there. First thing was to back to open my journal and record the day's four-chord concert.

It was hard to write under the *Comment* heading "RH only, conflicted feelings, must think of recomposing - not decomposing."

I could stand beside my organ and write in the journal on top of the filing cabinet and that had been my whole focus - to keep faith with my mentor of so many years ago. I looked sideways along the keyboard and out the window beyond at the light from a fading sunset. *Nice,* I thought. *The window faces north. Steady light. But maybe I should put a protective towel or something over the end of the organ anyway to protect the wood from the light.*

I'd returned from the bathroom with a bath towel and draped it over the end of the organ top, holding it in place by setting the weighty brass light for the music stand, on it. The door opened behind me as I fussed about keeping the towel spread protectively and moving the metronome to the other end of the top of the organ.

"Good evening Mr. Scottman," said a heavy-set matron in a yellow tunic and pant uniform that reminded me, except for the colour, of the institute from which I had just been released. "I'm Eva. I'm your PSW. I've come to get you ready for bed."

I reached to roll down the cover over the keyboards. The red eye saying I had not turned off the console, glowed still. I switched it off, checked that my earphones, on the shelf at the right end of the keyboard, would clear the covering and then let the lid rattle softly down into place. I guess one of the kids put them with the pencils when they saw how startled the Administrator was. I reached in my pocket for my key to lock it and realized I had no keys, no wallet, no phone, not even my Day-Timer with my schedule. My breath caught.

Where are they? I thought in a panic, *my keys, my pocket collection.*

My eyes must have been darting around the room in alarm because the lady stepped back quickly and shot a glance into the bathroom. She quickly closed the door to the hall to reveal another door. She snapped on a light switch.

"Here they are, I think," she said and beckoned me across the room.

There, in a room-sized closet, was my dresser, the sturdy arm chair from my wife's grandmother beside it, and on top of my dresser, lined up on the antependium I had rescued from a church that had long been torn down, all the stuff I carried in my pockets. I breathed a sigh of relief. I went over to touch them just to be sure, counting as I did so; flip-phone, pen, Day-Timer, keys, wristwatch, wallet. I touched my face to be sure my glasses were in place. Seven items - all there.

I realized suddenly the presence of the woman behind me and that I had rather rudely ignored her. I turned and waved a hand at her.

"I'm sorry, I don't recall your name or why you're here," I tried to say but it was just garbled nonsense.

She repeated her introduction with a smile.

I raised my eyebrows and hands to ask what a PSW was or did.

"I'm one of the low-priced-help here." I followed her as she backed out of the closet and back to the organ. "I make sure you can get yourself together, shower twice a week at least. I also nag you if you depart from the straight and narrow. Any bumps, I help you over." She smiled broadly.

"My first job is to get your bed ready."

That is when I realized that there was no bed in the room - just the organ and the filing cabinet. She reached high on the wall where my audience had been standing and pulled a latch and down dropped a narrow cot. I had to back into my entryway to be out of the road.

The bed was all made up complete with pillow and the quilt my wife made the year before she died; it was for a double bed and was too big for this one, but it had been folded up on the sides to fit into the recess in which the bed fit. Now Eva dropped it down over the edges of the bed to the floor and folded the bedclothes back.

There was a narrow walkway down each side of the bed. A wooden flap folded out at the head of the bed.

"This is for a book you might be reading in bed," she flipped on a recessed lamp, "and the well in the shelf is to secure a glass of water if you need one. You are the only one in the place with a bed like this," Eva said. "You even have your own sheets."

I was a bit dazed.

"So now you have to get into pyjamas and let me see if you can manage getting into bed."

She must have sensed my start at having to undress for her approval.

"I've seen it all before, Mr. Scottman. Let's start by getting your sweater off."

I didn't move from my hallway. She stood aside as I struggled to pull my sweater with one hand, and then shrug my good shoulder out and catch the garment as it fell off my stricken arm. It caught on my hand.

"Well done, young fellow," Eva complimented.

She reached to retrieve the garment from my disabled hand. Then she watched me unbutton my shirt and shrug out of it.

"We'll be sure your shirts are pre-buttoned for the biggest opening, so the sleeve slips on and off your wrist. I'll cut off other buttons if you want."

She slipped the shirt off my wrist and led the way into the walk-in closet.

"Laundry in here," she said dropping my garment into a lattice cylinder. "Let's see you get off that undershirt."

When I successfully put on my pyjama shirt under scrutiny, I waved her on her way to suggest I could manage my pants by myself. She agreed and exited to bring my bedtime meds.

I always wear my pants for several days. I only have three pair - all dark grey. They all match my suitcoat, but they must be hung up to let the wrinkles fall out overnight. It is the practice of a lifetime and my next challenge. It took a while to lay my trousers over the back of my chair, smooth the legs flat down the back and onto the seat and then pinch the cuffs between the spring-loaded bars of my hanger. I hung them on the lower right hat hook of the hallway mirror that had been in my grandfather's house and which Donald must have moved from my bedroom wall at home. It was good to see another friend. I looked to the clothes rod beside to see their mates waiting under wraps from the cleaners, suitcoat next, six ironed, white long-sleeved shirts next tuxedo in the garment bag beyond. My son had to have included the rack of ties beyond as a joke. Rakish and open-necked would be my new style.

By the time she returned I had done the teeth and toilet routine and was sitting on the bed she had turned down.

"Breakfast is after seven and until nine. You are not on the room service list," Eva said as I laid back and she flipped the quilt over me. "Here's the call button if you need help during the night." She pointed to the softly glowing switch hanging over the small bookshelf. "And if you are not up by nine, I just fold up the bed with you in it. Got it?" she enquired.

I gave her a thumbs up salute.

"You've done really well, today, Mr. Scottman," she said softly. "Welcome to our humble abode. Sleep well."

She smiled and stepped out of the room. The door clacked gently behind her.

I should have asked her to tell me a story, I thought. I don't know how long I lay staring up at the ceiling, weakly lit by distant streetlights shining through the window. I don't think it was long.

4
UNMADE DECISIONS

I left the breakfast table well-satisfied and on a mission before physio was scheduled. The Administrator would have what I needed. Sure enough, I saw it on her desk as soon as I opened her door. I didn't ask, I just picked up the pad of Post-it notes and waved good-bye as she looked up from her computer.

She leapt up in a flurry and a call for me to, "Wait!"

I stopped in mid-stride. I was about to get reamed out for my rudeness and steeled myself for the rebuke. Instead, she paused to scoop something from a noisy box in the second drawer down in her desk and caught up to me in a few steps. She handed me a pen; I already had my own and was about to write her a note but decided to do it by sign language.

I pointed at her computer and then at myself and raised my eyebrows.

"Your son said he'd bring your computer in today and hook it up. Is that what you wanted?"

I nodded and put hands together in thanks.

"You'll need this," she said, "at least for a little while until we assess your speech training and recovery." She handed me a metallic clicker, "You pinch the strap of spring steel on the bottom and it makes a loud click."

I recognized it immediately but hadn't seen one since I was a kid. Now I know why; she had collected them all.

"This is for your phone calls," she explained. "I spoke to your children, so they know what to expect if they call you. I told them to ask you *yes* or *no* questions.

You reply into the mouth mic with one click for yes and two for no. Three clicks are an emergency. All the staff know the drill so you can use it if they call your room intercom. I've told them to use your phone number in preference, but you never know. Understand?"

I clicked my toy.

"Now, did you sleep well?"

Click.

I raised the pad of notepaper and lifted my eyebrows.

"No problem," she said as she looked at the black band on her wrist. "You're due in physio. Go," and she shooed me in the direction I'd been told when I left breakfast.

There must be a heart beneath that armour, I thought as I retreated.

*

I have heard others say that it takes three weeks to form a new habit. In all the examples they used to illustrate their point, they were talking about something in their control. They lost weight or walked to work or stopped smoking - stuff like that. I can now add to that list a new group of experiences. It also takes about three weeks to accept changes forced upon you; I found I just got tired of griping to myself about them.

In my case, it is the damage of the stroke. My left arm will not work again, my speech will never be more than garbled sound, but I am getting more dexterous with one arm and feet at the organ. I have a callus on my thumb from using my clicker. Everyone calls that progress. But is it progress that will let me return to my house? That is the hard part and coming to accept that might take longer than another three weeks.

If I go home, my whole day will be consumed with the routines of living. I will face repeated problems making things work with one hand, dealing with appointments by telephone, getting to and from the grocery store, pharmacy, anywhere else, getting repairs done or the lawn cut. My musical life will slowly die under the weight of all those other things. When I say it that way, I think I've already decided. I'm going to take up their offer to stay here at Eternalcare.

The curious on my hallway took no time at all to visit my room and admire the organ. I fell right into the celeb trap without even thinking. I showed off some of my party pieces, first on earphones, then on low volume speakers when the group got to three; they'd all come and sit on my bed like kids on a church pew.

I amped up the speakers when the audience overflowed into the hallway on seating, they stole from the dining room. We enlisted those with walkers to load up chairs and push them down the hall after lunch or dinner. Our administrator got complaints from the staff. The audience was leaving the chairs in the hall after the recital. And some along the hall didn't like organ music; they wanted peace and quiet, *please*. Things really hit the fan when there was a medical emergency and the paramedics couldn't get their stretcher down the hall because of all the chairs.

So, I have accepted the solution to move my organ to a corner of the dining room. Moving partitions block it off and they hide me when I practice using my earphones. Everyone has been told not to bother me when I am in there. When we do a recital, the partitions move aside, and we have lots of chairs for any who want to come and we don't have to move them back. And the peace seekers have stopped complaining. So, a new life is spreading before me. To take it up, I have to face the litter of my last life living at my house.

On Sundays, the corporate bus takes me and any others who want to go, to Church where I continue to play for the service. They didn't reduce my honorarium because I can only use three of four appendages. Sunday afternoons

are the time I've set to deal with life's unmade decisions
still hiding in my house. The bus driver gets me a burger
and fries at a drive-thru just before he collects us. He
drops me at my house on the way back to the Residence.
One of my kids picks me up no later than four and takes
me back and stays for supper. I can call for an earlier
pickup if I need it. If I die on site, I'll only be there for a
couple hours before I am found. Everyone seemed to be
satisfied with that arrangement.

My key slipped into the front-door lock as it has for fifty
years. I stepped in; the house was cool despite the heat
outside. Today, my target was to take down the paintings,
portraits, sketches of all the musicians I have collected
over the years, and any other pictures I want to save. I
turned out of the hallway into what used to be my music
room. It had been a formal parlour in the generation
before mine. Women could retreat there while the men
adjourned to the companion room across the hall for
cigars and brandy. My Music Room has sliding doors to
both the hall and Dining Room that I used to close when
students came. Today, they stand open highlighting the

gaping hole in the panorama that my organ used to occupy.

The pictures I committed myself to take with me today are the ones that the Residence says I can have on the wall in my bedroom as long as they fit the dimensions of the wall. They also have to fit into my son's car in one trip. I turned in a circle to face the host before me. These are the giants of the classical musical world. The walls are covered, rank on rank, from shoulder to ceiling. Is there any point to counting them? No. Only a few can come with me. How do you choose? I slid into my castered desk chair to spin and admire them all.

As I scanned the gallery of the great, my mind drifted to the music in my library from each person's pen. Maybe that is how I chose; I take those with the most music in the filing cabinets below the photos and in the boxes in the garage and basement. How about the ones I've played the most? How about the ones I really like best? How about the ones I can still play without one arm? I felt myself sliding off an emotional cliff and got up to walk around the house.

I lifted from their hooks, a bunch of family pictures in other rooms - our wedding photo, a collage of summer pictures my wife made when the kids were young, the kids' graduating pictures, and our last anniversary picture. I stacked then along the wall by the front door and went back for the historical pictures of our ancestors, the ones who came here in the mid-nineteenth century.

My son made me a collage of all the cathedrals where I'd played the organ during our travels. I'd usually contacted the resident organist and asked if I could visit while we were on holiday and they usually allowed me to come in and play a piece of two. Those photos were like notches in a gunslinger's belt. But the frame was too big for me to manage with one hand. It should fit into the car, but only barely. I put a Post-it note on the pile to remember to take it.

When I looked at the stack on the floor by the door, it was already what the car could hold. There was no room for any of my musical mentors. I called for a pickup. Just calling Donald 's number was the signal he needed to come and get me, but he asked when he answered anyway.

"Want a pickup?" he asked. "It's really early."

Click

"Be there in a few minutes."

Click.

He found me in the music room with tears in my eyes. I was right; It took all Donald 's skill to get what I had chosen into the car without poking holes in something. Donald had opened the door and I was about to get in when I stopped. I went back for the portrait of Johann and the light over it; it was on canvas. Donald handed it to me to carry on my lap once he had buckled me in. I couldn't go back to the house for several weeks after that.

5
BIRTHDAY GIFT

I filled the walls of my walk-in closet with my family photos; the closet felt claustrophobic with so many. Mr. Bach and the cathedral collage got the wall over the filing cabinet, facing the window. The wall where the organ had been was bare above the skinny new table that stood in for a desk. It was enough to support my desktop computer. A printer was underneath where drawers usually were. I could see Mr. Bach from my bed, but the empty wall was the symbol of my inability to decide and it taunted me. I thought nobody knew until the kids came over for a birthday celebration.

There was the usual cake and ice cream in the Dining Room mid-afternoon. I was busy playing some old theatre organ music part of the time. That must have been when they went to my room to install my gift. They made an announcement to all in the room when I finished, that we should all come to my room. So, we did and there it was. Donald had photographed every face on the music wall and from the individual photo files, made a wall-sized banner - a collage of them all. The room shrank two sizes in appearance. It was a mob of my mentors from time and space compressed into that billboard on my wall. I was flabbergasted.

I came up to the palm-sized prints of each composer. It looked like a stadium of people from the playing field. At arm's length I could see each name, each face. I couldn't help running my hand across them as I walked along the wall looking down and up each row and column. There wasn't one which didn't call up a melodic line or moment.

All I could do was shake my head in wonder and hug both donors.

Donald then showed me how to call up each individual photo on my computer screen. The composer's name and dates were already there. Wolfgang stared back. Suddenly a parade of portraits began to cycle from one to another, flashing a new face every few seconds.

I waved my hands frantically to get them to stop. None of them deserved to be flipped away like some scrap. Rudeness like that should be reserved for TV commercials or billboard advertising.

"No, wait. Stop, Stop!" I tried to say.

Donald hit a button then a few more and said, "Is that better?"

From the computer screen, bespectacled Franz Schubert glanced sidelong at Donald who sat there with his hand on the keyboard. Franz seemed to be asking how he got there. I breathed a sigh of relief. Donald showed me how to tap a key to advance to the next photograph which stayed there till I wanted to change it. Bob Schumann was looking at Donald with equal uncertainty.

I signed to go back, and he hit the reverse arrow. Mozart eventually returned.

"You can type in the name if you want to jump the queue," Donald said.

He showed me how to move a cursor to open a part of the display on which I could add notes like the person's compositions I played, or stories I knew, or memories of events that featured the composer. He showed me using the file for Johann; it was fabulous. At last I had a real use for this machine whose only function had ever been to type out the weekly comments I made about the prelude and postludes I played at church.

When I went to bed that night, I had not felt so comfortable since I left home.

*

I never asked where the original pictures that had been on the Music Room walls went. I guess I was afraid to know. It was enough that they lived with me still in miniature or by magic in the machine on my table and broadcast on my wall.

Since childhood, I had collected my music books and sheet music as well as signed copies from composers. There was a lot - I mean a great lot. Any time I needed a new piece over the years, I had bought it and charged whoever as part of the cost of preparing for the concert. I was called a musical hoarder and I confess; I was.

When I started giving mini concerts or recitals at continual care, I would go home and collect the music or books I needed and bring them back to my room. The filing cabinet was already full but with the wrong music of course. I started to stack music and books in boxes and loose in my closet. Eventually, the Business Administrator called me to account. I could not store so much paper in my room. It was a fire hazard. I could have a single filing cabinet but that was it.

Got any suggestions? I wrote on a whiteboard for Eva to read, - *about the music?* I waved my hand to the offending pile that now had flowed into my bedroom beneath the window. I was sitting, back to Bach, in the rocking chair my wife bought me so long ago. It now occupied the corner across from the window; from there I could admire my gallery.

"Buy the place and change the rules," she said over her shoulder as she tucked in sheets and folded up my quilt.

I tossed my head.

"I gather you don't want to burn them?"

My eyes bulged at the insult.

"I thought so. You people with such limited imagination," she concluded from the other side of the bed.

I watched her tip up my bed and then she turned to look at me. She flicked her eyes up to my wall of fame.

"Can you make little copies of the music?" she asked. "If you could make them small enough, you could keep them in a dresser drawer. But I'll bet you want to use them again. Well, make up your mind; do you want to use them or keep them?"

"Out of the mouth of babes …"

I snatched up my smart phone and texted Donald, *Can all my music be scanned?* I pecked out.

A few minutes later, my phone chimed, and a message appeared on the screen.

"Get the Business Admin & call me back on speaker phone."

"The answer is yes; you could digitize all your music, but it will take a person with no other job probably months to complete the task. We'll have to hire someone - *you* will actually. There will be lots of money from the sale of the house so if needed, you could borrow several thousand against that. But why not ask the Music Department at the University if they will take the collection and digitize it in payment? Some graduate could get a thesis out of this, you'd get a copy of the music in a manageable format, and the house gets emptied for sale. I'm afraid the alternative is a dumpster or shredding service."

"I think that's being a little dramatic," said the BA when she saw my horrified response to the alternative. "I think your Dad has the answer he sought. The music can be digitized if he hires someone. Would you set up a meeting with the Music Dept. Head at the University?"

Donald sighed. "Sure. I'll go for something next week. Could you sit with Dad in the meeting? "

The BA agreed and they penciled in possible dates. My mind spun with how this would happen. Where do you start? Could it be done in the house? Would the music, the actual pages, follow the path of the pictures and disappear as they had?

6
GOING DIGITAL

I have no idea why things take so long to happen. The
meeting with the Music Dept Head came off just before
the summer ended. When my collection was described,
and then viewed by the curatorial staff, a polite letter of
rejection was sent to me through the Business
Administrator. That's when I decided I could not bear to
see all those scores, thousands of hours of musical
pleasure, disappear into a dumpster. I called my kids.

Sometime later, a graduate student appeared at
Haveyouforgotten Care. The kid was there before I was
called to the meeting and stayed after I left. She said she
could run a scanner and suggested that anything this size
could be organized into a spreadsheet that would allow

multiple means of accessing the material. I guess that is code for such a thing being an aided memory method.

She said she was in need of accommodation. Well the house was empty and fully furnished and all the material she would be working with was there. Donald said we should sell it right away but to do that, the works that were to be preserved would have to be moved to somewhere else or ditched. Maybe she could live there and pay a nominal rent that would cover the taxes? I left that for the others to work out. I got tired writing.

*

So it was that Jessica Turnbull took up residence in my house with two girlfriends, Trudy Brewer and Margaret Price. They immediately called to mind a movie Donald had brought over a long time ago. This trio would be Scottman's Angels. They were all pretty, dressed in jeans and T-tops, short hair, blond, blond, and brown.

Their combined reduced rents covered taxes, heat, light and water. There was no land-line telephone, TV, or cable. Donald arranged for unlimited internet and the ladies said that was quite adequate to their needs along with their own cellphones, which they pay for themselves. I insisted that Jessica keep a record of the hours they spent daily and promised a supplementary bonus beyond the credit offered in the token rent and payable in a lump sum when the task was complete. For the cost of this project, I had budgeted what I'd pay tradesmen to do a workmanlike job.

Jean bought a super-duper scanner to digitize, that's what they said it did - digitize - the various pages of music. What an absurd idea - that music could be reduced to a series of numbers. Music has long been my example of something being greater than the sum of its parts. However, that is the descriptor attached to this process. I don't have to like it, just use it, but it still is an indicator of the linguistically challenged society within which I live.

Jean bought two computers and some cables and boxes also on my credit card; one computer was dedicated to run the scanner plus a serious backup system. When I got to my house after church one Sunday, the air tingled with ozone from Margaret and Jess working their way through a stack of files of music. While I had only hired Jessica, she seemed to have subcontracted the others to share the load and the pay; I hadn't thought about that. I work pretty much alone and just assumed most others did as well. Here was community in action. And they seemed more than excited about the project. When I saw how well they worked, I decided I had to up the estimate on labour costs. If I'd gotten any peripheral lesson from the musical mentors in my life, it was how most of them were exploited. I would not be party to that. Nevertheless, seeing the budget triple only made plainer to me the cost of keeping stuff about which I had not made discriminating decisions for half a century.

Tough, I thought. It would be paid for by the capital gain on the house. I jumped back to pay attention to Marilyn

"I worked in the library over the summer," she said, "and when I heard about this job, I asked my boss for tips on how to do it properly. The first step is to make a catalogue of all the titles. That database can be augmented with notes about the significance of the book, availability, condition, all that sort of thing."

Margaret was entering her work into the second computer that Jean had purchased for this purpose alone along with the hardware to hook it to the backup system.

"I just had to imagine all the ways these books needed to be organized - by what criteria would they be compared? Jess and I worked on that. She wonders if there is a thesis out of this."

"Have you any idea how many books or manuscripts are here," she asked looking at my bookshelves.

I dug out my portable whiteboard.

"Ask yes-no questions. 1 = yes; 2 = no." I held up my clicker.

She read my scrawl.

"More than 500 books?" she asked.

Click

"More than …?"

I held up a hand to interrupt her and left for the kitchen. I returned with the yardstick that hung from the nail on the back of the pantry door. I measured the length of a shelf. I realized suddenly I would be using English units she did not know. These kids were raised on metric. *Tough,* I thought.

I wrote the length of the shelf on my whiteboard - "Forty-eight inches."

I pointed to the shelves in both cases as I counted them and wrote the number on the board - "Sixteen." I computed the number of shelf-inches in these bookcases.

I then held the end of my yardstick to a bunch of bindings in sequence, waggled my hand, and wrote the average width of a book - "one inch at most."

Trudy wandered in from the other room to observe the calculations.

"Are you saying there are likely almost 800 books here in these cases?" Trudy said open-mouthed.

Click. I rolled my hand to suggest we move on and pointed to the back of the house.

"And more in the garage?"

Click. Again, I rolled my hand to continue as I pointed through the floor.

"And more in the basement?"

Click.

"Oh my ..." She cut herself off deciding I might be offended if she swore.

"Do you think, all together, there are more than two thousand books?"

Click. I rolled my hand to signal her to guess a larger number.

"More than three thousand?"

Click.

"Four?"

I waggled my hand.

Margaret jumped back in with her estimate of catalogue time. "If I can do five an hour by the time I move it onto the desk for appraisal, examine each for marginal notations, note the Table of Contents, special items in each book, enter the relevant material and bibliographic reference details into the computer and then back onto the shelf, that will take me"… I could see her labouring under the calculations. Five an hour would be an optimistic estimate.

I wrote on the whiteboard and then pointed to her. I turned to the other's then added similar numbers for them. I circled the total, then added, "400-500 hours, Sch yr = 34 wks, 2x 8 hours/weekend/student."

"This will take all year to finish," Trudy concluded.

Click.

Trudy went to talk to Jessica about her epiphany while I returned the yardstick to its nail.

*

When I stopped by the house, the clutter of documents in progress through the digitizer had been shoved to one end of the table. In solitary splendour, at the open end was a tome that lay like a stone tablet. Seeing it there made me anxious. An unmade decision made so plain.

The book was a handspan thick; Its cover was thick and solid - carved wood under tooled leather. Prominent was the embossed title, *Illustrated Holy Bible.*

"We found this in one of the boxes in the basement," Margaret said.

You had to admire the craftsmanship, the gilded edges of the pages, the pronouncement its size made. I flipped the cover open with a *thunk*. On the elaborately decorated frontispiece was the date with decorations to match. Victorian.

Page after page of etchings stared back as I turned deeper into the musty depths.

Garden of Eden, Joseph Receiving His Brothers, Crossing the Red Sea, Moses receiving the Commandments, Noah on Mount Ararat, Samson at the Temple, …Florid, fanciful art illustrated mythical stories like photos in a tabloid. Roman numerals numbered the pages. The girls, looking over my shoulder, could not decipher them. I wrote down how you figured them out. Large print you might read from arm's length, declared the text written in the day when King James I commissioned it more than four hundred years ago.

In the middle of the book, where there were usually pages to record family births, deaths, and marriages, were the stumps of those pages; they hadn't been sliced out with a sharp knife, deep into the crease, but torn out roughly leaving peeks of the red and gold border that had once enclosed those names.

More engravings depicted moments when cameras didn't. *Jesus in the Temple, Jesus Feeding the Five Thousand, Saul on the Road to Damascus.* The squalid life of Biblical peasants was buried beneath heroic poses and incredible vistas.

The gilt edges of the pages were completely unblemished. Not one fingernail had caught a loose page to scratch the patina of the surface. There were no marginal notes, no bookmarks, no record that anyone had looked at this since it had been presented to … someone … somewhere. There was not a single smudge or print from an inky finger, not a single corner folded down to make finding a passage easier.

Someone bought this for an anniversary or special event. Maybe it had been donated to a church when it opened or after a renovation - a prestige presentation to mark a donor's piety. The evidence was that it had rarely been used. The torn pages suggested it might have been part of a family's stuff that fell into indifferent hands when a senior died. How it had come to be in my music collection I don't know. I had been given music from many church organists over the years; maybe it was sent on to me by mistake, buried in their leftovers as it had been in mine. Maybe it had been sent on so another didn't have to figure out what I had to now.

The removal of the pages suggested I not jump to conclusions. Someone wanted to save what was on them. I'd guess they were young because they didn't know how to slice the pages out with a razor.

When we came back to these pages, I mimed how the removal should have been done with a razor blade to slip them free.

"What do we do with it?" Margaret asked.

Silence. I hooked my thumb over my shoulder.

"But it seems so wrong," Trudy interjected.

I pulled over a piece of scrap paper, *unused for 100+ years*. I turned up the etchings and shook my head at the depictions.

"Could I have the pictures?" Trudy asked.

I stepped into the kitchen and returned with the sharp paring knife and showed how to cut the pages deep into the binding to remove them. I mimed how she could frame them in something from the Dollar Store.

I turned away as I heard the zip of the knife doing its work.

7
TEST RUN

I did my best to ignore the blank wall behind me, the wall of missing persons, as I danced around the girls who had finished their first run at the contents of the top drawer in one filing cabinet. Jessica had just noted that every copy of sheet music had dates in the margin.

"Are those pencil dates in the margins, the dates on which you played those pieces?" she asked.

Click.

She called to Trudy to ask about dates in the margin of the music books she was cataloguing.

"Every one," was the reply. "He sure made a lot of notes," she quipped.

"Ha, ha," Marg replied in a bored voice.

"Those are the dates of performance, or when they must have been used as background information," Trudy continued. "We better add that to the spreadsheet. I didn't think of that, but it might be important to know that later and by then it will be too late to go back."

"That will slow me down quite a bit," Margaret replied. "Most of the margins are well marked up. But if that is what you want, it will be part of my drill."

As Trudy and Jess chatted and fiddled with the columns in the display, Margaret shuffled the files she had, preparing to go back and add the dates they had not included on the first run.

I pushed over my whiteboard with a new note. *Put things back in place and order please - so I can find them.*

She smiled and nodded. I sighed.

As I pulled each item off the shelf or out of a drawer, I stood a cardboard marker in its place.

Margaret clarified that the many markers she could see in the drawers and between books on the shelves were for the files that I still had at Perpetual Care.

"You should bring those files to me so I can catalogue them. Then I'll put them back, otherwise they will get missed. Can you do that?"

Click.

I added a smile and heart pat in thanks.

*

I had real apprehensions about the digitizing project, but I bit my tongue and went along with the plan. It was after Thanksgiving that I was asked to come and do a test run. My daughter joined us on the Sunday afternoon; they sat me at a keyboard.

"Enter the name of a composer," Jessica said.

I pecked in *Bach*. A list of his works appeared in an index.

"Pick one," she said.

Toccata in D min.., I hadn't finished before a new menu appeared. I tapped the choice that said, *original score* and up swept Johann's copy. I back arrowed and chose the alternate. My own copy with the dates in the margin appeared. The over-arrow opened the score to the first page and successive taps moved through the score in orderly fashion. I back arrowed to the first page again.

We went through selecting several other works. In each case a menu popped up with all the copies I had in my library, even references to the books that held commentaries or background on the shelf. I could select any in the list and instantly the first page popped up. It worked just as it was supposed to.

I went back to the main menu and I found I could select by musical period, calendar date played, or date of composition. I could select by nationality, even key signature. The team was clearly proud of their work; I could find anything in the database faster than I ever could before.

"I think we nailed it," Jessica said to the others.

How do I point out the problem? I wondered. I waved to get everyone's attention and went back to my first selection. I put my fingers on the desk as though they were playing a keyboard then looked at all them for the sound effects. I held up a hand to indicate we'd do it slowly.

On the first bar they came in, raggedly with the organ-like hooting sound. I nodded to keep them going as Trudy put a finger on the screen to follow the notes. I moved my feet as though I was playing the second bar and the bass notes from there to the bottom of the page where I stopped and reached dramatically to tap the keyboard to advance the score to the next page.

Jessica got it immediately, "He can't advance the screens without pausing; he needs a switch."

I gave a thumbs up.

"There are foot switches for that; pianists use them all the time."

"Look how busy his feet were without reaching for another switch."

"Could we mount a switch on the bench that he could nudge with an elbow? Have you any muscles in your left arm that could twitch to operate a switch?"

The ideas came thick and fast.

"Course we could always resort to a page turner?" someone suggested again.

Jean interjected, "He used to solve page turning by taping paper score pages into an accordion that I spread across the whole music stand when he prepared a piece for a concert. But that would need paper copy and the aim was to eliminate the paper."

I waved a hand across my throat.

"Let's think on that," Jessica said as I wrote out my compliments on the database and the way it was organized. This was a good job. I drew a big star over the whole whiteboard. This would work. This could advance with another year's worth of effort.

8
THE CHINA

I left the data team and beckoned Jean to follow me through the sliding doors to the Dining Room. In the corner, were a pair of handsome china cabinets that had come from a century before. They were wooden framed, dark with age. Glass panels let light through the doors and sides to dance around the curves and colours within.

I'd added glass shelves in one cupboard to support teacups in display mode, rather than stacked in pairs or nested in quartets on deeper shelves. With the extra shelves, the capacity was triple that of the original case. In retrospect, my efforts to put more cups where few had been was the thin end of the wedge - the first indicator of a juvenile Stuff Saver; a collector of unmade decisions.

Fifty fancy teacups were spread out on those shallow shelves for the admiration of all. Assorted crystal bowls holding cream and sugar sets fought for space. Cake plates commemorating an empire now gone, stood in nested rows on edge along the back. What used to be the admiration of all was the source of incredulity to the women who now occupied my house. They had worked around these cabinets without really studying them. I wanted to show the stuff off now. They'd never seen anything like it.

"Well…outside a museum," Trudy had admitted.

She's right. I'd been living in a museum. In the second cabinet was silver tableware from both my wife's and my parents. There were stacks of ornamental, vases with grape-clustered decoration, pitchers, serving trays, tea and coffee pots, matching cream and sugar containers. Only I knew they were there. Each item glowed with the patina of age beneath a brown flannelette cover of, *silver cloth,* so called for the silver dust that impregnated the fabric. The dust oxidized into black silver oxide, tarnish to everyone else instead of the silver items being darkened. All you could see through the wrinkled air-tight plastic wrappers were non-nondescript lumps.

When those things were new, plastic hadn't been invented so each piece had to be polished regularly. Tarnishing was caused by the home heating season and the Sulphur released by the coal burned to warm those homes. By Christmas, everything came out and was polished with rags from old shirts. And again, by Easter, spring cleaning started with another polishing before the family feast.

Dominating the second case were the candlesticks. There were enough candelabra to require a fire permit if they all were to be lit nowadays. The last table they graced was probably twenty feet long - it stretched from this room through to my music room. There were twenty-two candles in all; I couldn't recall the last time any of the pieces, besides the candlesticks, had actually been out of their shrouds.

Here in these display cases was the evidence of success -
the silent statement of frugal living that allowed beautiful
things to be accumulated piece by piece over a lifetime.
You saved and pinched pennies till they squeaked to
splurge on things like this just so you could display them
on a feast day and be admired. Some of those items
represented years of careful planning and parsimony; that
was not their only message, if you could understand what
they said.

These items on display stood testament to the chests of
silver cutlery and serving utensils hidden in the caverns
of the china cabinet across the room. In those long
drawers and end hutches were the tablecloths and linens
for a table of twenty-four along with the gilded china
place-settings that were the foundation of every bride's
trousseau for three generations. These were the storied
symbols of community, the record of adversity
overcome. And I didn't know what to do with them.

When the students came to live here, the dining room was treated with the reverence of a shrine when they first arrived. The dining table was what caught their attention because they were thinking of a place to spread out the paper from the filing cabinets and boxes they had to catalogue. It stood glowing from its lemon-oil polishing.

"You could play ping pong here," Jessica had said as she surveyed the space. "Look under here," she said urging the others down to floor level.

I didn't need to see the massive legs with their ornamental, dust-catching fluting; I knew better than anyone else in the room, the double set of legs that held up the leaves that could be added to extend the table. Those four boards stood hidden behind the china cabinet ready to extend the table another six feet.

The interest in the table as a work surface had prompted Jean to immediately pull open a drawer and flip the quilted pad, that belonged under the table cloth, over the table, followed by the plasticized black tablecloth Marie had made. Her mother had taught her well.

The cleared table stood amidst the cabinetry waiting for the next round of digitizing.

"Should we add some of the leaves to the table?" Jean asked. "They may need more space…"

I shrugged and waved towards Jessica, suggesting Jean ask her if she needed more space. It would come at the cost of traffic space. They had pretty well used up the walls by the time they moved the eight chairs that had been nestled under the dining table, out to the walls between cabinets and into the music room where the organ had been. That added to the space they wanted to spread out paper, but it did make for sideways walking through their workplace. It would make a splendid stretch, but probably out of place anywhere else but a room like this, these days.

I ran my fingers along the padded, plastic-covered tabletop as I walked around to study the cabinets again. I couldn't recall the origin of most of those teacups. I know that had been gifts or saved from one estate sale or another. Each one had a tale, but I had lost those stories now; there was nothing written down. What difference would those stories make if you didn't know Aunt Leathy or Minerva Cordelia?

"That one came from Esther Georgiana, did it not?" Jean asked from my elbow when she saw what I was admiring.

I nodded.

"That is a name from a novel," said Margaret who had broken away from the others and joined us.

"She was my three-G aunt on my mother's side," Jean said.

"Three - G?"

"Great, Great, Great Aunt, sister to my Great, Great Grandmother. She came to a farm in the wilderness with her husband and worked her way up to being able to afford to give something like that as a gift. She gave it to my great grandmother as a wedding gift. Every time I see it, it tells me I can succeed through hard times, if I work at it."

"Next to it, the pink Coleport porcelain, is the one from Minerva Cordelia, my G Grandmother's sister. She's the one who stood by her sister when her sister lost her husband in an industrial accident. An iron casting fell from a bench and cut through his boot. "Just a scratch," he said when he got home and looked at the injury. Two weeks later, he was dead of blood poisoning; no antibiotics then. Just at Christmas it was. So, Minerva Cordelia came to town from the States to live to support her sister - just up and sold her home, dragging her husband along as well, because her sister really really needed her. That's heroic; that's a model I want to remember. So, when I leave, I want to take those two cups."

"Her sister, my grandmother had two preschool children and was then a widow," Jean continued. "How did you keep food on the table? There were limited chances for a widow with children to earn a living … respectably. MC showed G-Grandma how, by investing the small amount of money she had, in mortgages. That brought in a quarterly income she could count on. She also helped GG run a boarding house and vet those who got to stay there. That covered day-to-day expenses."

"Is there a story like that for everything in this cabinet?" asked Margaret.

I nodded slowly - pulled out my small whiteboard and scribbled, *used to be - forgotten now*.

Jean added that when the story is gone, it is just a small and pretty teacup that won't go in the dishwasher and in which your tea cools too fast.

"So, these cases are really like an archeological site where the documentation got lost."

I nodded.

"But the one I'm working with over there," she hooked a thumb towards the bookcases of music, "has the dates and places."

But stories only I know! I wrote on my board.

"He has a journal of every performance, every service he ever played for," Jean interjected, "with a comment section. That's as close as he got to writing the stories."

"Well maybe those notes, if you'll pardon my pun, would remind you of the story."

Too slow to type, I scribbled.

"Maybe you need a ghost writer?" Margaret said tentatively.

I shrugged.

So, what do I do with all this stuff? I wondered again as I scanned the shelves. *Call the family, then the antique dealer, then the second-hand shop, then the dumpster,* Marie used to say. *What's the point if no one knows the story?* I remember asking.

Well that's pretty arrogant and egotistical, she would have said. *How do you know yours is the only story that could be written with those things? Maybe they just need to find a new home.*

And I would have said, *so, the Antique shelf and the secondhand store are orphanages for stuff - things waiting for adoption?*

That's a nice way of saying it, she would have said.

Jean broke into my reverie, "Shall we go back to your place now? It must be teatime."

I turned towards the hall where I put on my coat in front of the mirror that wasn't there while Jean said our thanks for the successful test run on the archiving project and our goodbyes. I picked up the material I'd collected for next week's concerts and church Order of Service and was waiting when Jean got zipped into her coat.

9
CONGREGATIONAL SOUL

"Eva tells me you spend a lot of time preparing material you give me to send to the church secretary to put into your weekly Order of Service," said the Business Administrator as she accepted the memory stick I gave her.

I nodded. I think the Business Administrator is really trying to battle her dark side; she is always dressed for royalty and the suits seem to come with a haze of rules she has to squint through. Every so often I think she takes a big breath and tries to blow them away. I had that feeling right then. She'd accepted my device and looked about to scowl her *not again* glare when she actually snapped her mouth shut, closed her eyes, opened them and smiled at me.

"I've read some of what you gave me to send in on other weeks. It is really scholarly and stresses a lot of techniques and … is it musical theory?

I nodded again.

"Why do you do that? Aren't you just a church organist?

I chuckled and smiled as I looked down; I wrote on my whiteboard, *really want to know?*

"Let's talk in the Dining Room," she said as though spirits in her office needed to be escaped from.

When we got there she asked, "Would it be easier to type on the keyboard to your organ computer and let the words appear on your screen?"

I went to the bench, shoved over so she could join me, and propped the computer keyboard on the lower keys of the organ.

*Minister **thinks** he owns congregational mind*, I typed. *I **know** I own congregational soul.*

She smiled.

Windows show off light and old stories; I show sound - teach how to hear - join them to listeners around the world since time began. It took a long time to peck that out and when I finished, I added, *and I'm humble too.*

"Are you doing that in your concerts here?"

I nodded.

"Tell me one way you do that?"

Key signatures carry emotion, I pecked, then went looking for a graphic I used with some students. I played the scales that started with each of the coloured notes and cued her response to the emotion's others thought they felt by pointing to the faces. After a few, she seemed to get the idea.

Key sets tone for whole service. Minor keys = sad, plaintive. OK for Lent, Good Friday. Major keys = happy times.

Again, I played different major and minor scales to illustrate my point. Then I played more examples and she guessed accurately which was which. *People know - feel it.*

"What ..."

I held up my hand. *Can't type enough.*

"Will you type out a guide for concerts here as we continue?"

I nodded. *Since she suggested it, she could hardly object if I moved some of my book collection into the library - for resident education, eh?*

10
THE CHOIR

When I bought my three-manual organ, I put away the electronic keyboard that had been my practice instrument; the girls found it, in its original box, in the course of sorting the basement and garage collection of boxes of music. They had asked if I wanted to take it with me to the Extensivecare. I got Donald to bring it when the Business Administrator was away, and the day it arrived, we started our first choir practice.

All the organ stops and a bunch more were accessed by buttons and a dial on the keyboard. I couldn't play the left hand and there were no pedals to substitute for the low notes; all I played was the melody line in the right hand. It was all that was needed for the group who had suggested it. If we could manage to sing melody together, that would be a good start.

So, we started with one of Mozart's most famous melodies, *Ah vous dirai-je Maman.*

"I don't speak French," one prospect complained immediately when I showed the title on the top of the photocopies I handed around.

"I forgot my glasses," said another who seemed to be there under protest but was following his wife's wish.

Each of my inductees had a printed copy of the music, single staff, large font. While they fussed, I played through the melody.

"I know that," said the man without glasses. "Why don't we sing that?"

I pointed to their scores.

"But that song isn't French - it's English," said the lady with the language issue.

I played the first two bars of music on their page as I pointed to the notes on my screen over the keyboard. I looked at them, opened my mouth in an *Ah* and played the first note holding it while I looked at them with raised eyebrows. I waved my hand then played it again. Everyone joined in. *Pretty good* was conveyed by my nod. The first note was repeated, and we quickly got two separate sounds for the same single note.

We stopped and then tried the jump between the second and third notes. It was the interval I wanted them to get. We had to go back over that interval several times to get everyone to make the same leap at the same time.

We got to the sixth note and I held it. They all knew to hold it - that was the way the song went. I just wanted to make sure they recognized that the open note symbol meant that it was to be held compared to the black notes that were not.

Only when we had completed the melody to *Ah* did I let them start with the words - English words.

"Twinkle, Twinkle, Little Star …" they sang energetically.

I drew a deep breath, held up a finger and managed to communicate that they were to sing that line with one breath. And then we did it loudly and softly, each time showing the markings that would tell them to do so. It was the former history teacher who translated for the lady who didn't speak French, that the loud symbol 'f' stood for forte, and the 'p' stood for 'piano' which meant quietly.

So, we larked about with this for ten minutes or so before I changed to another key to sing the same piece - again in unison.

When we managed to get it in the new key, and they could do it without the keyboard. I pointed to three to go back to the starting key, while the others sang the second melody. They stopped after three notes in amazement; they were singing in harmony!

And so it went. After half an hour, my choir of rank amateurs could sing their first concert piece in two-part harmony. They knew note values and pitches and were thoroughly pleased with themselves.

To give them a break at the end and to bring some fun into what a demanding half hour had been, I played the embroidered variations that are a party piece. I had to fling my feet around soundlessly to play the pedals that weren't there, but they all got the message. It was a review of expression and note values; it signaled the way

I was going for their next meeting by playing the minor key variations which made them all squirm.

Everyone left laughing, singing in harmony all the way down the hall on their way to teatime.

By the time the Business Administrator caught up with us, it was ten days later and it was the full-voiced performance of a chorus of twelve in two part harmony that she'd been invited to in the Dining Room after lunch and before naps. I watched her in a mirror set up above the music stand. In a distant day, I used it to tell me when the offering had been collected or the bride had arrived.

Here I was watching for the facial telegraph. She answered the call with clipped steps that got her barely into the room. I didn't wait; I called for the 'forte' version and she was stunned. She was shaking her head by the interlude and all the wind was out of her sail before we finished the French verse. I could see the *there-he-goes-again* look flash across her face before it was replaced by a smile. I think it was Mrs. Pekot's presence that really tipped the scale. Tania is from the Memory Suites section.

She applauded into the expectant silence and then said, "I'm going to book Carnegie Hall," and left.

She didn't ask me to get rid of my piano.

11
RECIPES

It was during a search of my basement music storage for
material, that the ladies unexpectedly came across the
box of cookbooks. I'd forgotten I'd put them there.
Maybe I didn't. Maybe the kids put them there when they
cleaned out the kitchen prior to the arrival of the students.
The Evercare Bus had dropped me at my house after the
service. After I handed my just-used material back to the
digitizers, I went to find what I thought I needed for next
week. I'd pointed to the boxes I wanted to look through
and Margaret had hoisted them up the stairs and onto a
cleared corner of the dining table for sorting. When I

opened the first box, there they were - rank on rank of cookbooks, ragged with loose paper sticking out of them. It was not what I expected.

While Trudy and Jessica continued their perfected ballet with my music scores and the electronics, Margaret diverted her attention to scan this new trove. If it looks like a book, Margaret is helpless within its sight.

The kitchen library had been stacked into the box, spine up. ***Good Housekeeping, Julia Child, Joy of Cooking, Northern Cookbook,*** were the fat volumes separating wads of pamphlets on the top layer. With their removal, a packet of letter-sized sheets in plastic archive folders that had been stuffed down the side, fell over onto the lower layer of pamphlets. Margaret pulled it clear and couldn't help noticing the title on the top page, peaking from beneath the rusting pinch clamp that held the clump together. ***Gingerbread Cookies***, it said in bold print. I sighed.

"Look at this," she declared as though she had found Tut's tomb.

"There goes the afternoon," I said to myself. I wanted to put the books back in the box and get her to lift the other box from the floor, but Margaret had the bit between her teeth and there was no stopping her now.

"Look at this," she squealed again running into the music room waving the pages. "This is a real gingerbread recipe for cookies." She was wide-eyed and riffling the other pages in the collection. "And here's one for Shortbread - must be a dozen variations. Look! A recipe, no two, for Light and Dark Christmas Cake. My God! This is the Mother Lode!"

CHRISTMAS CAKE INGREDIENTS
LIGHT CHRISTMAS CAKE
1 lb butter
1 lb fruit sugar
8 Egg
5 Cups sifted Flour
2 lb bleached raisins
1/2 lb fruit cake fruit

1 lb assorted coloured pineapple wedges
2 lb red & green cherries
1/2 lb blanched almonds (slivered?)
1/2 cup fruit juice or wine

Directions. Makes about 10 lb (3 x 2 1/2 lb plus 2 x 1 3/4 lb)
1) Soak raisins overnight in juice/wine
2) Cut up pineaple, cherries into slivers or small chunks (Easier to cut cake later) (takes 1 hr) Save few
3) Cut up almonds or buy slivered almonds, cherries, pineapple, or nuts to decorate top
4) Line loaf pans with 3 layers of brown paper (LCBO bags) (takes about 1/2 hr while watching TV)
Start in large Mix Master bowl & transfer to LARGEST MIXING BOWL (yellow Tupperware)
5) Cream butter well and add sugar, then eggs and flour
6) Switch to large Tupperware mixing bowl, add raisins, nuts, fruit cake fruit. Separate lumps of raisins
7) BY HAND, fold in cherries, pineapple. Mixing gets really hard by this point
8) Divide into pans so each cake is about 1-1/2 to 2 lb. Decorate top of each cake.
9) Bake at 275F in 2 lb cakes. Takes 2+hr till skewer comes out clean and surface is slightly cracked. Cool 15-30 min. Remove from pan, & carefully peel off paper. Cool on rack overnight. Tea towel cover
10) Inoculate lightly (repeatedly?) with Sherry. Wrap in Freezer wrap. Store in Cold Room or freezer.

DARK CHRISTMAS CAKE
1 lb butter
1 lb Brown Sugar
3 lb Raisins (2 lb Sultana, 1 lb Seeded)
2 lb currants
lb glace cherries, - Red and green
1 lb pineapple
1/4 lb preserved ginger
10 eggs
1 lb Blanched Almonds (slivered?)
1 lb mixed fruit cake fruit
1/2 cup Sour milk or Sour Cream
1 cup Black Currant or Grape Jelly
1 Tsp each :Cinnamon, Nutmeg, Cloves. Mace
1 Tsp each: Lemon, Vanilla, Almond Flavour
1 Tsp Soda sifted into 4 Cups Flour

Directions Makes about 13 lb (4 x 2.75 lb cakes plus 2 x 1 3/4 lb)
1)   Cut up pineaple, ginger & cherries into thin slivers or small chunks (Easier to cut cake later) (Takes about 1 1/2 hr while watching TV) Save few cherries, pineapple, or nuts to decorate top
2) Cut up almonds or buy slivered almonds
3) Line loaf pans with 3 layers of brown paper (LCBO bags) (takes about 1/2 hr while watching TV)
Start in large Mix Master bowl & transfer to LARGEST MIXING BOWL (yellow Tupperware)
4) Cream butter well and add sugar
5) Add and stir in eggs one at a time
6) Add sour cream or milk, flavourings, spices and jelly

7) Add flour (with Soda in it)

8) Move to Tupperware bowl. Add raisins, currants, Fruit cake fruit, Nuts. Separate lumps of raisins

9) Fold in Cherries and pineapple and ginger. Mixing gets really hard by this point

10) Decorate top with slivers of saved cherries, pineapple or nuts

11) Bake @ 275F in 2 lb cakes about 2hr 15 min - skewer comes out clean, surface slightly cracked. Cool 15-30 min. Remove from pan, carefully peal paper. Cool overnight covered with Tea towel on rack

12) Inoculate lightly (repeatedly?) with Sherry. Wrap in Freezer Wrap. Store in Cold Room or freezer

GINGERBREAD COOKIES If the dough is prepared ahead of time, this is a great activity for children from age 2 onward. Do not try to make a double recipe. Make 1 recipe twice if needed

Preparation time: about 25 min.

Chill: 2 hours at least. (Can be made a day ahead)

Bake: about 10-15 min. @ 350F for 2 pans

Makes about 30 cookies each about 2 ½ inch diameter and 1/4 inch thick.

Ingredients:

1 Cup packed brown sugar

1/3 cup oil or shortening (If you use oil in the measuring cup first, the molasses won't stick to the cup)

1 1/2 cup dark molasses

2/3 cup cold water

7 cups all-purpose flour

2 teaspoons baking soda
2 teaspoons ground ginger
1 teaspoon ground allspice
1 teaspoon ground cinnamon
1 teaspoon ground cloves
1/2 teaspoon salt

Instructions

1) Mix brown sugar, shortening, molasses and water in large bowl. Stir in remaining ingredients. Cover & refrigerate at least 2 hours.

2) Heat oven to 350F. Grease cookie sheet lightly with shortening or Pam.

3) Roll dough ¼ inch thick on lightly floured waxed paper (too much flour makes cookies hard and dry) or between pieces of waxed paper. Dough comes out uniform thickness if flat wooden bars (rulers) are placed on each side of dough and the roller runs on them as it presses down the dough. Cut with floured cutter and place 2 inches apart on prepared cookie sheet. If cookies stick in cutter, wash clean, re-flour, and try cutter again. Better to have a bunch of cutters at hand. Keep dough chilled by removing small pieces from the refrigerator to use at a time.

4) Bake 9-12 minutes @ 350F depending on size or until no indentation remains on surface when lightly touched. My small boy/girl cookies take about 8 minutes to cook. Overcooking makes for brittle cookies which have to be dunked in milk or coffee to soften. Remove cookies onto

wire rack to cool. Decorate with coloured frosting if desired. Half recipe made about 40 medium gingerbread men

1 cookie (no frosting): Calories: 195 (from fat: 25); Fat: 3g; Cholesterol: 0mg.; Sodium: 135 mg.; Carbohydrate 40g.; dietary fibre 1g.; protein: 3g.
1 Cookie (with frosting): Calories: 220, Carbohydrate: 47 g, other items as above

Decorator Frosting
The following recipe can be made in fractions or divided into portions and each coloured differently.

Mix 2 cups (500 mL) icing sugar with 2-3 Tablespoons (20-45 mL) water & colouring - just enough to make the icing that can be used easily in a decorator's tube. Or put some icing in a clean white envelope, fold the sides and snip off one corner to make a decorating tip.

Tips on Gingerbread cookies

1) My rolling pin is an 18" (45 cm.) length of hardwood doweling, 2" (5 cm) diameter. To roll out the dough ¼" (6mm) thick I place the dough between two scrap strips of laminated flooring 1/4" thick, about 2" (5 cm) wide, and about 15-18" (35-45 cm) long and roll the roller on the strips while spreading the dough.

2) When I make up a recipe of dough, I divide it up into 7 balls, each the size of a snowball or baseball

(hardball). Each ball is placed on a sheet of waxed paper about 24" long. The ball is placed about the 8" mark and the paper is folded over the ball so the ends match. This puts the dough ball in the center with the waxed paper on each side.

I squish the ball down with my hand then continue with the roller (supported by the wooden strips mentioned above), starting from the patty of the ball and pushing the roller away to the edge. I then rotate the waxed paper ¼ turn, put the roller into the center of the dough again, and push it away. If you find the dough spreads almost to the fold of the waxed paper, turn the package another ¼ turn and roll away again to avoid splitting the fold. A couple finishing forward, and back rolls of the pin and the package is ready to put into a tied plastic bag in the fridge to harden up.

 When I take the dough out, hours to days later, the dough will be 'stuck' to the waxed paper but that can be peeled back on both sides and floured so that it doesn't stick any more. Re-flour the paper as needed to keep it from sticking to the dough. Children like to sprinkle the dough on the paper with their fingers. Keeping the dough between waxed paper keeps the rolling pin clean and keeps the dough from drying out in storage.

I start by giving each dough patty a couple more rolls to take out wrinkles. It the dough got flattened too thin, flop it over itself, or squish it back into a

ball and re-roll. Keep rolling down to a minimum –
it tends to make for harder cookies if a lot of flour
from the paper is worked into the dough

I also get out only one 'ball' of dough at a time.
Cold dough is easier to cut up into cookies than
warm dough.

3) Children need to be trained to put the cookie
cutter into a small bowl of dough each time and
then on the 'edge' of the patty of rolled out dough.
They will want to put their cutter in the middle,
leaving less space for the next cutter and resulting
in much more re-rolling of dough scraps. They
also need guidance to line up cookies on the
greased cookie sheet. There should be a finger's
width between cookies on the sheet before baking.

4) Scraps of dough are squished back into a ball
and re-rolled into a new and smaller patty. Floured
hands and a lightly floured paper surface help to
keep dough from sticking.

5) A 'ball' of dough will make about one large
cookie sheet of cookies. Make larger cookies first,
and then use up scraps for smaller cookies. It is
best to serve children several small cookies rather
than throw out a large one with a bite taken out.

"Stop!" commanded Jessica, who was focused on keeping paper coming out of the scanner in the correct order. When she had got her own stack safe, she turned.

"What?"

Margaret was already handing Trudy pages.

"I always used to have gingerbread cookies when I was a kid but when my parents split up, I never learned how to make them myself. Dad was a strictly store-bought type. These look like the things my Mom must have made."

Jessica took pages handed to her.

"What's the big thing about Christmas cake? Who likes that stuff?" and she scowled at the page, stained by use, that stared back through the protective covering. I guess she was used to looking for dates on everything after cataloguing the music.

"Mr. Scottman are these your wife's recipes?" she called back to me.

Click, Click.

"Where did they come from?"

I had to find my whiteboard, *Chauvinist*! I wrote. It took a moment to sink in.

"Yours?" Margaret gasped.

I nodded.

"Did you really make these things?" Margaret repeated waving the sheets. She was so excited; it was hard not to smile.

I nodded again.

"Oh, Mr. Scottman, could you show me how to make these things?"

This had obviously touched something deep in her. How could I say no? I nodded and signed that it would have to be some time in the future. I took the pages from her and pointed to the ingredients. I hadn't seen any molasses or baking soda in the pantry - only soups and boxed foods. They ate a lot of fruit and raw veggies. Then I pointed to the Instructions where it said, *"Mixing gets really hard by this point"*. She followed my finger down to the page where it described how to roll out cookie dough between a pair of slats that made sure the dough was even thickness and opened my hands in query about where the rolling pin might be.

She marched immediately to the kitchen and began opening drawers, "Here they are," she called. I followed her. Sure enough, the drawer was as it had been since my wife died. Nobody had moved a thing. On a guess, I opened the cupboard below, and signed for Margaret to look at the back of the bottom shelf. She hauled out a stack of Tupperware.

I took the pages from where she'd dropped them on the counter and pointed to the instructions that said *transfer to LARGEST MIXING BOWL (yellow Tupperware)* and then to the ingredient list in the Gingerbread Cookie recipe -**_7 cups_** *all-purpose flour* then pointed to the large yellow plastic bowl part way down the stack.

She pulled it out in triumph. When she stood beaming and looking for a place to put it amidst the clutter on the counter, I held a hand in caution. I made a mixing motion with my good hand and pointed to her.

"Got it," she said. "I have to do the mixing." She checked the recipe sheets again, "So, when can we go to get the stuff for the cookies?"

I checked that the drawer still held the slats beside the wooden rolling pin. I mimed using cookie cutters on the counter. That set off another search. We found a labelled can in the pantry, top shelf, beside the washed and nested collection of Tupperware canisters that had held sugar, and flour back when. Sure enough, the flour scoop was still inside with the set of Tupperware measuring spoons and cups and the Pyrex, two-cup pitcher.

When those items came out, I could see the old MixMaster standing under its plastic hood at the very back of the shelf. On the shelf where we couldn't see them until we got up high, wrapped in a plastic bag, were the worn wooden spoons needed for mixing heavy batters and wire cooling racks for cookies. We proved the mixer still worked and then I suggested, with a note on my whiteboard, that we might arrange for one of my kids to take us to the grocery store the next Saturday. Margaret was just dancing.

*

It was a truly thrilling experience to see Margaret turn into the Baking Barista that she became.

"I'm also putting on weight," she said. It was probably the wedge issue that eventually separated her from the other girls.

I didn't complain. Her baking became yet another reason to come round to the house to pick up music. It was a trip down memory lane for me, to come into a house smelling of sweet things; not something you got at Nevercare where calories were counted with a miser's touch.

The first Gingerbread Cookie lesson was slow but that was because I had to spend time on the basics.

Dump the flour into the measuring cup, then scrape the overflow off level, I showed her.

Don't dig flour out of the canister - you get too much, I cautioned on my whiteboard. *Bottom of the meniscus on the line for liquid levels, I pointed out. Level measures on spices*, I demonstrated. She sucked it up like air from the room.

I thought I had remembered everything until the sheets of cookies went into the oven to bake and I couldn't find the oven timer. Margaret used her telephone alarm. I showed her the touch test for doneness. She forgot to set a timer on the last pan and found out how over-baking makes for crispy cookies - *dunkers* she called them. I wondered if they should be called *travelers*; they would survive any trip.

12
BRAD

Brad Daniels sits at my table for meals now; he's just moved in and there was nobody else at my table, so he was seated with me. He was always conservatively dressed, like me. Maybe it was an interior decorator who suggested that fitting us together made a fashion statement. I heard that the Business Administrator had clued him in on my speech problem.

"He writes answers to your questions, so he's kind of slow," she had said.

"Probably as well," Daniels replied. "I don't understand very fast."

"I think you two will get along fine," the matchmaker had replied - well that is what my PSW, Eva, said happened.

Mr. Daniels has chronic heart problems - COPD his doctors say. And he has mobility issues as well. That seems to be a post hip replacement problem.

Cross-threaded! he wrote on my whiteboard. We were both dawdling over tea.

"That's what it feels like. Every time I step forward with my right foot, there is a jolt in my hip."

High-priced help? I wrote again.

"In a never-ending parade," he replied.

"Each one sends me to the next and I arrive and wait to be sent back or to another of that one's friends, or to get another pill to add to my collection. It really makes me think their job is to keep each other on a payroll. It seems my place in the process is to say I have a pain somewhere or other. Once snared, you never get out, nor does anyone want you to."

Cynic! I wrote.

"Your turn is coming,"

Can't write fast enough, then added, *Ask Y/N questions*. I held up my clicker, *1=Y, 2=N.*

Daniels squinted at my scribbles and laughed. When he got to the end he looked up.

"Know any good music?"

Click.

"Stroke?"

Click.

There was a long pause, "Need a page turner?"

Click.

I picked up my pen, *Read music?* I wrote.

He squinted at my question. *Snap*, he replied with a flick of his fingers.

I smiled and waved him towards the organ in the corner. I left the partitions in place so we should not be disturbed. I slid over a bit so he could join me on the bench and flicked on the organ and the widescreen monitor now on the music stand in place of the music usually spread there. I handed Daniels a pair of earphones and put on my own. While he fiddled to get his wire clear of me and the keyboards, I tapped in a command on my small wireless computer keyboard. Up came Felix's Wedding March.

I had to tap his feet with mine to get him to move a bit so I could reach that end of the pedalboard. I reached up and tapped the lower right corner of the keyboard that would change to the next page of music. When I tapped on the left side, it went back to the first page. I opened my hand with a *Got it?* motion and raised eyebrows.

"Oh, I do, I do, I do," Daniels fluttered and puckered up to kiss me.

I nudged him in the arm as I backed off a bit and nodded to the screen. Away we went.

"Tah, Tah, te, tah …," he said as we launched slowly into the piece.

I read ahead so when I got close to the bottom corner and was about to move my head back for the nod to turn the page he was already reaching for the corner. He tapped it right on my nod.

I continued down the page wondering if he'd see it and was gratified when we got to the double dots that he tapped the left corner to go back to the start of the repeat.

130

He was right with me on the jump to the second ending. He sat back, his duty done, and I drifted down the page to the end. I held the chord.

I looked at him with raised eyebrows and waved to the screen.

"I used to sing - small stuff - part of a bunch of choirs over the years, caroling at Christmas - that sort of stuff. I still can't make those black notes into sounds in my head, but I know when you're playing whatever notes. I was surprised when I noticed the repeat dots but remembered them from the other page so that worked well enough. Thank you for playing slowly for my benefit. Now do you want to try it *a tempo*?"

I smiled. *I could like this guy,* I thought. We went through my planned work for Church and the afternoon concert for Eternalcare. By then it was teatime. I signed for a cup.

"I appreciate you letting me turn pages," Daniels said with a sigh. "I get to feeling so lonely lately. It's probably a tincture of some neurochemical I've stopped making but it is really hard to deal with. So, coming here to listen to music that was part of my life and pretend I am helpful, boosts the morale a bit."

I put a hand on his arm and went back to the screen. I played to the end of the page and then reached up to touch the screen myself. The stop and start were obvious. I put a hand over my heart in thanks then switched off the equipment. He gave me the earphones he'd been wearing, and we retreated to the tea cart which had rattled into the sitting room across the hall behind us.

The biscuits they serve at tea come from the metal box in which they are sold and probably came from the mill that rolled the steel for the container.

As the first shattered between my teeth sending a cascade of crumbs, into my lap, I thought of Margaret's *travelers*

- the declared failures. *How can people sell these things?* I wondered. I wasn't alone.

"Do you think they make these things that way or are they so old that they've fossilized?" asked Brad.

I stood abruptly and held up hands to say he should stay seated. I'd have taken him to my room, but I think steps for him were painful enough to be counted. My room was just a moment down the hall. I returned with my survival pack from Margaret. Standing so others could not see, I offered the plastic bag containing her gingerbread cookies - the real ones, the prize winners.

Brad's eyes lit up and he immediately understood the reason for subterfuge. He took one and set another on my saucer, sealed the bag and tucked it into the pocket of his walker, out of sight. He could have been a magician from the speed with which it happened.

I sat down with my back to the room and we each nibbled on our delicacies. He took off the headfirst; I, a leg. The cookie broke gently between my teeth, a waft of molasses drifted up my nose, a tingle of ginger on my tongue.

Brad was doing the same, his eyes closed to shut out distraction.

"Hmmmmmm," he sighed. "I'll ask about your secret supply later when we're out of camera range," he muttered without moving his lips.

I gestured inviting him to tell me about himself.

"I've had a few 'incidents' lately," he said bracketing the words in the air. "They told me that if I took any more like them, alone in my apartment, I could die. So, I bit the bullet and decided to die in public. At least if I take an attack here, someone might see me before I decay." He finished his cookie with another satisfied sigh.

"I have no family nearby," he continued. "My companion died a while ago."

I nodded in acknowledgement.

"You have children?" he asked.

I held up two fingers.

"Boys? Girls?"

I wanted to hold up a finger on each side until I remembered.
I held up a finger on one side then moved my hand across my body and held it up again.

"And your wife died a couple years back?"

I held up one finger.

"And it took six months to have a stroke?"

Click. I flipped a hand towards him to ask about his partner.

He confirmed what I'd asked and then pulled out his phone. He sat purse lipped as he considered what he was about to tell me.

"My companion was a sculptor. He loved wood," he said. "We met a fellow sculptor in Africa; he carved this using my companion as a model but wearing a local chief's outfit."

After a long look he passed the phone to me.

He's gay, I immediately realized. *I wonder how big a risk it was to tell me something like that?* I reached out to pat his hand and nod as I gave back the phone. I tried to give a *no problem* wave. I think his return nod was acknowledgement of my indifference to who his partner was. To have lost a soul mate was tough no matter who they were. I pulled up my whiteboard.

Sorry, I wrote. *How did you clear out your place?*

"He took liberties, but it really was a self-portrait. He died a long time ago," Brad said.

"He went out after we came home one night, said he was going for a drink. The police called me next morning to say he'd been found dead. The rent money in his wallet was gone. I think it was Fentanyl. It was just appearing around here at that time. Whether someone put it in his drink, or he was looking for a high and got a contaminated batch, I never found out. He just went out and never came back. Don't think I ever got over it."

His voice faded on the last comment, but he revived to continue. After a moment he seem to remember I'd asked him a question.

"So, to answer your question, I packed two suitcases, one for seasonal and one for off-season stuff. It's easier to make the decision fast and then don't go back. And it's even better if you do it all at once. When they came for me in the company bus, the driver took my bags down. I loaded up Jonas, here, on my walker," he waved to his phone, "and walked him down in the elevator. From my room here I called the disposal company my lawyer uses, and they cleaned out the place to the paint. I think they sent whatever was recoverable like furniture or dishes to one of those second-hand stores, I have no idea. The clothes, and refrigerator stuff went right into the dumpster."

"Cabinets full of letters and manuals and tax filings - GONE! Library of books I guess I enjoyed but couldn't name unless I pulled them out - POOF!" His hands exploded apart. "I listed the condo for sale, and it was gone two days later with the money in my bank by the weekend."

I shook my head in amazement. He'd handed the decisions to someone with the objectivity of a banker to decide what had value and what didn't - someone out of the loop, someone with objectivity and who knew the routes to others who needed or wanted whatever it was. But among those criteria, the story that went with anything was worthless. That seems rude, … irreverent, …disrespectful… wrong somehow.

"Isn't that what you did?" Brad asked with a laugh.

I shook my head emphatically.

"Did the kids move the organ?"

I nodded.

"So, what was left?" Then he caught himself. "Ahhh, the Music!"

The tea wagon was being collected. We were expected to return our teacups. I stood and beckoned him to follow. I put our cups on the wagon as we passed.

When we reached my room, I let him follow me in so that he couldn't see my wall of fame until I stepped aside.

He glanced up in silence, then swiveled his walker so he could sit down. I put my diminished cookie collection into my dresser drawer then came back to join him. His head flipped back and forth like the carriage on a typewriter.

My Jonases, I wrote on my whiteboard.

"A lot of them were gay you know," he said.

I nodded.

"Kids make that?"

I nodded.

"Nice. No way I know that many people."

"Was the rest of the house like that?"

I sighed loudly and nodded.

"Sorry," he said with sincere sympathy.

"So, I'm guessing you've been converting your music library to a digital format?"

I nodded again.

"And you'll be tossing all that paper soon," he presumed.

I looked to the ceiling in despair, hands beseeching any deity for release from such a future.

"Is there something rare in all that paper?"

I shrugged.

"You'd like there to be because it would mean it was worth saving all that time? It would justify the mountain of money you spent assembling it."

He had it, I guess. I acknowledged his analysis with a grimace. He was cutting pretty close to the bone but what I had been doing could not have been done with less. I was training a generation to hear what they were listening to, to join with people they never met in an experience of the heart. Surely that was worth what I had assembled.

Brad was reading my mind.

"I've noticed what you do for the concerts here. You want people to appreciate subtlety and nuance in a day of loud and repetitive auditory assault."

I was nodding and smiling. He did get it. But the way he said it made me feel like I didn't belong - like I'd blundered into the wrong party at a hotel.

"The stuff that you accumulated to let you teach that appreciation then, might not be what anyone else needs to reach the same goal. Your stuff has done its job. Whatever is in there is available on-line now. So, it is alright to let it go."

So comforting, I wrote. *Now I feel foolish.*

"It's the symbolism," Brad said, "all the good memories. But they'll last if we keep the image. By the time the pictures are forgotten, we'll all have greater worries probably."

How could anything be of greater worry? That took me a while to write out; it looked so desperate on my whiteboard.

He patted my dead arm.

Could I have forgotten how quickly I'd lost the use of my arm and speech? Was he saying I'd forget my passion to make music to share because something else was more important? How could that ever happen? Would I lose my caring when I lost the emblem of my effort?

13
UNEXPECTED DISCOVERY

Every couple of weeks when I'd return to the house to put back music or books that I'd used or to pick up more, the girls had some unexpected treasure to display. The cookbooks had been one; from a basement box of music this time had appeared a silver trophy cup from another age. When I got there, it had tipped over on some music. It was child sized. The prize winner was T. Cowles according to the Gothic script. The date was September 9'11 - over a century ago.

"It was dinted when we found it," Trudy declared pointing out the fingernail depression below the inscription.

"Well it says it was "won by" so it was presented after a competition," she continued. "What's it doing in with this box of organ music?"

I looked at the rest of the music in the box. I pointed to a bunch of score titles and the dates of printing at the bottom of the page.

I scribbled on the box. *Victorian Church Organist - music judge?*

"Well that would make some sense," Margaret said. "If he was a judge, this was the cup that was presented - but not. Do you suppose it wasn't given because it was damaged?"

"Maybe the kid left and forgot it?" Trudy suggested.

"If he left it, the organist would have sent it by mail, I'd expect," Jessica chimed in. "It might have been expensive to do so but it was the right thing to do. My guess is that it was damaged, and then a replacement was made so this was left over. What do you do with a damaged trophy? I don't think you could take the dint out? And it had already been inscribed."

"What kind of music competition happens in early September?" Margaret asked after some thought. "Kids have just got back to school. Nobody is ready to play anything unless they practiced all summer."

I picked up the cup and turned it in the light admiring the patina of age on the silver.

"Could it be a trophy for something else, like baseball?" Trudy suggested.

"Wouldn't you see a team name on it?"

"Maybe he was best pitcher or hitter or something. Maybe his Dad was the organist and it just got misplaced."

147

"Did they have baseball in Victorian times?"

"Why was this box in your basement, Mr. Scottman?" Jessica asked.

I gave the universal *I-don't-know* shrug. *Was Organ Society Pres. once.* I wrote on the whiteboard now that I'd found it while they were talking.

I lifted a few more scores from the box to get to a pair of tattered paper-backed books that were face down in the box.
On the back of the top one was a list of the pieces inside. I scanned the list and knew what the title would be. I turned it over. It was. I handed it over to Margaret who laughed and read it out.

"Twenty-five Organ Selections for Funerals," she declared. That got laughs from the others.

I held the other, still face down, and waved my hand around the circle to guess what this one's title would be. They all were a bit confused. I urged them with my hand.

"Well I'd bet the title could be Twenty-five Organ Selections for Thanksgiving," said Trudy.

I pointed to how dog-eared the edges were and shook my head. I waited for the others.

"Weddings," guessed Margaret and I turned it to show she was correct.

"There were a lot of weddings, more than funerals, judging by the wear." noted Jessica.

Late brides, I noted on my board. That took a moment to sink in.

"He had to play the book over and over while waiting for the late brides," Margaret interpreted.

Trudy had been looking through the Funeral selections. She came to an envelope glued inside the back cover.

"Look," she said and pulled out a sheaf of five-dollar bills, all pressed flat by the weight of paper and time on them and all with King George staring up at us.

I wrote on my whiteboard, *George VI - 1936, I think, till 1952. Cup belonged to organist's father.*

"Eighty-three bills," Trudy reported, "all fives."

"Look in the wedding book," Margaret said and reached herself when the others were slow to react.

Inside the back had been a similar envelope. You could see where the glue had stuck to the cover and the cover had been distorted by a fat package. As the pages shifted, two ten-dollar bills fell out of the book where they might have been tucked like bookmarks.

"Well it cost more to get married, and there were more marriages after the war and the price had gone up," concluded Margaret with pride in her deductive skills.

Trudy gathered the bills together and handed them to me.

"These are yours," she said. "Your lucky day."

What do you do with found money? I wondered. *I didn't earn it. I didn't really find it.* It seemed like it should be shared. *How much pizza could you buy with four hundred and thirty-five dollars? More than I'd want to eat.* The Bible story of the Widow's mite used in the church service came back to mind. *What was plan B?*

I accepted the money then opened the book to remove the envelope in which most bills had been. With the money back inside, I slid it into my suit coat pocket resolving that we should have a party next week. But first the stuff had to go to a bank to see if it could be redeemed. *I'd better have Donald with me to do that,* I thought.

I was about the call Donald to take me home when I noticed the Cowles Cup was still on the table. I held it up. Everyone shrugged. What do you do with an old trophy?

Trudy picked it up and, in a step, opened the china cabinet, slid a saucer slightly and added it carefully in the corner opened by the move. I had hoped someone would take it as a pencil or pen holder, but these people didn't seem to use pencils much.

*

I got Donald to bring me over to the house the next Saturday night. Jean joined us. I brought the celebratory pizza the girls had ordered, ice cream with assorted sauces, sprinkles, and round coloured candies that the young person at the bulk store said were favourite add-ons. There was still four hundred dollars in the envelope in my suit coat pocket.

The pizza had hardly been served before Jessica produced a collection of drawings from the margin of the wedding book of songs.

"Want to guess about these?" she asked.

"Done by the soloist," suggested Donald. "The style is not antique. Maybe as she was waiting for her turn to come."

"I'd say the organist who got tired of playing while he waited for the bride to show up," Margaret suggested.

Child of person who brought box to me back when, I scribbled on my white board.

"How about this one?" Jessica asked.

"Definitely, the groom as seen from the music bench or choir loft," Trudy said.

"I'd say one of the ushers," offered Marilyn.

Father of the bride, I wrote.

Here's another. Different days/places, I continued on my board. *Female, student,* I wrote. *Focused hard on task. Look at the set of the shoulders,* I thought.

"Late student I'd guess," offered Trudy when the grand piano picture came up. They turned to me when nobody else contributed.

"Design for concert program," I wrote.

I knew this one. I'd put it there. I think it's back when I was just getting started. There is probably a copy in my journal.

It was ice cream time by then. The two cartons came from the freezer where they'd been waiting. Trudy bent a spoon trying to serve the first one. I got up and retrieved the proper scoop from the kitchen drawer. As soon as

Donald saw it, he laughed and announced that yet another relic from another age had just arrived.

I brandished the scoop high hoping it was the relic he referred to, not me.

"My Mom found this in a flea market?" Donald declared. "Look at it."

I gave him the weighty scoop with the self-cleaning bale that swept the bowl when you pressed on the geared lever that stuck out of the side. It had the tarnish of age going back beyond any of the young people there.

"Mom bought it for twenty-five cents because the bowl had a dint in it and the bale wouldn't swing. It needed to be placed over the point of an anvil and tapped gently to smooth it out and in five minutes the bale swung perfectly, and we had an antique worthy of the name." He passed it around for everyone to try.

Margaret got a nudge and a boo from the others when she declared the scoop, "really cool."

I didn't need to ask who would take the item home now that it had been recovered from the back of the kitchen drawer. I doubt you could eat all the ice cream that thing could scoop before it wore out.

They made things to last then - like centuries! *So much we made back then was like that and now we have to figure out what to do with those relics nobody wants,* I mused as I waited for my serving.

The left-overs pizza slices went into lunch boxes - they really used plastic boxes to carry lunch with them to work each day; the delivery boxes and bags were in the recycle and I was getting ready to go.

Trudy and Margaret had both struggled from the basement with boxes smelling slightly moldy and filled with more music to be catalogued that night. Judging from the dirt and dust adhering them, these boxes had not had my attention in a long time, if ever.

"More treasures," announced Trudy as the boxes hit the table with a double thud.

"Open them carefully," cautioned Jessica, "we don't need the dust all over the place."

I decided I didn't need to be here to watch this. Jean had already excused herself and was gone. I signaled Donald and he nodded.

We'd stepped into the hall and I was reaching for my coat when Trudy said, "Uh oh."

It wasn't the words; it was how she said them. She didn't shout them. They were hardly audible above the sound of the scanner Jessica was running across the room. The words were not the disgust of finding a dead insect or mouse below the pages she had removed. This was fear that I heard, and it went through the room like lightning.

I looked at Donald who had obviously sensed the same thing. His eyes were wider too. We both turned to look back into the dining room. Trudy was backing away from the box, a handful of music in her hand, and she was afraid. She bumped into the china cabinet which banged and tinkled in protest.

"What?" everyone seemed to say at once.

Margaret was closest and as soon as she looked into the box, her epithet was appropriate.

"Shit," she said and stepped back as she looked up at Jessica and then us.

"Sorry. I thought you had gone."

Donald was ahead of me, but he stepped aside so I could look into the box. In the depths of the box, wedged beside piles of yellowing music and brightly illuminated by the overhead light there was no doubt about it. It was a pistol.

"How did that get there?" Jessica asked when she saw it.

Margaret stepped up with her camera and took a picture of the thing in the box and then snapped off photos of the whole room from where she stood. With fingers flying, she emailed the pictures to herself at her school account and to the other emails she had of those in the room.

"What do we do with it?" Trudy asked.

"Where did this box come from, Dad?" my son asked.

I shrugged.

Trudy still stood against the china cabinet with the handful of music she'd removed from the box to reveal the weapon. I held out my hands for it. The yellowed pages were brittle. The top paperback book had a colourful cover that had been visible through the folds of the box. *Organ music for all Occasions* was the title. There were some pieces of music, not complete scores, just scraps. Most of the handful was newspapers from Chicago dated fifty years ago.

I held then out for Donald to see.

"Put them down on the table, Dad. I think we should call the police." His phone was in his hand and he hit the three-digit number.

Donald gave a one-sentence description to the operator and repeated our address. He was giving personal information when a siren came up the street. He told the operator that he was going to the door to let the police in and to please tell them what was happening because we didn't want to be shot.

The officer at the door stood well back and called Donald to come out slowly with hands in clear sight. My son passed the phone to the officer and backed away. A curt conversation between officer and operator finished.

"Are there more in the house?" the cop asked.

I could hear him talking but not what was said.
Eventually Donald called us out.

"Please come out slowly, one at a time."

When we were gathered, and the officer perceived we
were not a threat, he parked his gun.

"Sorry about that," a second officer apologized.
"We just got a call that it was a domestic call with a gun.
Too many buddies have come out of situations like that,
badly."

The first officer led the way into the house. Donald
pointed to the box.

The officer put on blue latex gloves before removing it.
He described the pistol to himself aloud. I wondered if he
was talking into the microphone at his shoulder.

"Thirty-two calibre, nickel-plated revolver," he said. He flipped a catch and the pistol opened. "Loaded with 5 unfired rounds." He removed the bullets. His partner came forward with a tough plastic bag and the bullets were dropped in. Another bag received the pistol. Both bags were set on the table. I realized when he turned around that he was wearing a body camera and was panning the room and table.

"Well," he said, "that's about all the excitement for now. It's drudgery time. We need to get a statement from each of you."

Two other officers suddenly appeared at the door. I could see that their car, with flashing lights, blocked the street. More conversations happened and two women officers joined the other four followed by two more with tackle boxes. It was getting jammed.

We should have sold tickets, I thought,

We each were asked to give a statement separately. We were all done when Donald saw the ice cream scoop still on the table.

"I need to add something to my statement," he said. "I recall getting that box at the same flea market the day that Mom bought the ice cream scoop."

I had not been with them at the time. He said his Mom saw the box and the music title through the space between the flaps and thought it might be something her husband would like. The kid looking after the booth took two dollars for the box, sight unseen, and they were on our way.

"I had to carry the box," Donald said. "Picking up the ice cream scoop brought the memory back."

One of the officers identified herself as a detective.

"Maybe you got a box intended for someone else," she said to herself but we all could hear.

"Are we in trouble?" Donald asked.

"You did the right thing. We have to investigate. We hand over our results to the Crown Attorney's office. They'll be in touch. Here's my card."

The girls each got one.

"Oh," said the officer, like she'd had an afterthought. "We have to take the box in which the gun was found along with the paper that was in it. It is evidence you know."

We all looked at each other.

"Could we send you with another box or two?" Jessica asked.

Madame Detective was not amused.

"Where can we get another gun?" asked Trudy as soon as the door was closed. I was glad to see she had recovered from her earlier shock.

"Well, there are still more boxes," Margaret suggested.

We watched the cavalcade of vehicles gradually clear the street.

"They never tell you anything, you know," Margaret declared as she turned from the hallway.

I went back in as Donald collected his coat. I noticed that before Margaret picked up the last dirty dishes, she first took her phone off the top of the china cabinet. It had been standing propped against the ornamental crest over the door and peeking over it.

"Jeez," she said, "got to charge that now for sure."

I tugged Donald's sleeve to get us out of there. I was whipped and I sure wasn't going to ask why she would need to video a police recovery of a gun from a 50-year old box of music.

14
CHRISTMAS

Margaret made Christmas Cake for gifts. She named it differently for each person she presented it to - anything but Christmas Cake. It was always well received especially by her omnivorous and ravenous male friends. She kept a supply in the cold room in the basement. I cautioned her to store it in the metal containers that bulk popcorn arrived in. She didn't want to attract rodents, did she?

Before they set off for Christmas, my three digitizers decided to have a special dinner. My children and I were invited. I think they were celebrating the clearing of the dining table. They had catalogued all the filing cabinets, and the basement collection. Only the garage remained.

With my wife's cookbooks and Margaret's new-found passion, it was to be a traditional affair with turkey, stuffing, squash and beans, fresh-made buns, Christmas pudding with lemon sauce. I was asked if I could bring out the candlesticks. We decided to limit the number to four otherwise we'd have to extend the table.

Jean got out the linen tablecloth; Donald brought a dozen candles to add to the half dozen still in the drawer. I was in charge of telling the story as I unwrapped them. And of course, I couldn't say a word. It all had to be hand-written.

Mom's I abbreviated on my whiteboard as I unwrapped one of the five-candle set. First off was the blue velvet decorator bag, gold braid-bound with tassels and protector of the plastic Ziplock plastic bag below.

Next came the brown silver cloth bag that enclosed each item. I waved to Jean to explain.

"The cloth is infused with silver dust. The dust has a huge surface area and so reacts with Oxygen and Sulphur in the air trapped in the bag before the flat surfaces can, so the silverware doesn't tarnish as fast. These bags are quite old now and should be replaced. They can't protect the silver anymore because the silver dust must all be oxidized or close to it."

By that time, I had the piece out, and the bag back in the sealed plastic. I took one of the old candles from the drawer and wrapped a strip of waxed paper that came out of one of the sockets, around the base. When done, the candle stood proudly in place. *Bigger candles back then*, I wrote on my whiteboard. I gave each of my admiring audience a candle to wrap themselves while I got out the mate.

When we were putting in the candles to the three-light candlesticks. Margaret pointed out that the bases were different.

"Is this the wrong mate?" she asked.

Minerva Cordelia's, I wrote. *Cheap or a fraud*? I wrote.
I looked to Jean again to take up the story.

"When Mom cleaned out her Aunt Minerva's
house as her executrix, this came to our house. It was in
pieces."

She pointed to the arched and curved rods that looped
from the base to support the sidelights. There was a hole
rotted through the base. It was a wreck.

The other," I had it out of its bag by then, "was so
black you couldn't tell it was sliver - well only by its
blackness did you know it once was silvery."

"Dad took it to a silversmith who repaired this
one." She held it up. "He used a base from another that
had been scraped and was in his pile to recycle. So, it
was close, but anyone could see it wasn't a match. The
silversmith reassembled the pieces of the other and then
re-silvered them both. They look pretty nice eh?"

"Why was there a hole in the base?"

"To add weight, a hollow base was usually filled with lead, to keep it from tipping over. Remember these things could light stuff on fire. Well some charlatan found that you could fill the base with cement instead. It was cheaper and the customer never knew - well until the lime in the cement reacted with the metal and rusted a hole. Aunty chucked it into a box probably intending to have it fixed but she died first. So, Dad had it fixed and each time it comes out, we review the story of a cheated forbearer and a right response by relatives who treasure her memory."

"Despite her being conned, she was still a stand-up support for her sister, my Grandma, when she needed help."

"That is a lot to remember from one candlestick," Trudy observed.

"The whole cabinet is filled with that sort of thing," Jean added.

"Some Stuff!"

The meal was as festive as any I could recall around that table and lit by those lights. Margaret was ecstatic about her new-found meal-making skill - just getting it all ready at the same time. We all complimented her, and I took all the Christmas Cake I could get.

When the candles burned down and it was time to extinguish them, Margaret, was drawing breath to blow out the first one when I touched her shoulder.
She drew back. I went to the cabinet and found the snuffer and showed her how to use it. Margaret continued around putting out each candle, studying each flame intently as it died.

"You've never had to get the coloured wax out of linen when it flies off the candle and spatters on the cloth," Jean said. "You used to use blotting paper on both sides of the cloth and run a hot iron over the spot. Most came out. Elbow grease took out the rest, but you had to be careful not to damage the fabric with scrubbing. We haven't got any blotters nowadays. So, you put a table ornament over the spot next year. But you always remembered how that spot got there; in those days, the tablecloths lasted a generation - at least - like this one."

15
THE PAGE TURNER

Margaret came to visit me at my residence at the end of Study Week. She brought a friend with a contraption.

They arrived while I was practicing and must have stood behind me watching as I went through the program for this week at Whocares Retirement Home. Brad was doing swim therapy, so I was on my own. I guess I'd punched a few page turns by myself before she cleared her throat to announce her presence; I didn't respond. I jumped a bit when I she touched my shoulder. Nobody bothers me. When I'm that far into my music and with my earphones on, I'd miss a fire bell.

"I have a friend who wants to offer a hand that can turn pages," she said when I turned and took off my earphones. "This is Sam," she said.

I put out my hand to shake. His grip was warm and firm.

Sam plays with me in the university orchestra. He's taking courses at the college actually and just comes over to play with us. He is keen about electronics; he made a gadget that he says will turn pages on your screen. Some of the musicians use it with a foot control. He's put in a light controller for you. Would it be alright if he showed it to you?"

I smiled at Sam and moved over. I had to move back when he came up on my right side. There was a chat and he installed some app wirelessly onto the computer running my monitor.

He set a black gadget the size of a match box on the thin casement under the lowest keyboard only a couple of handspans from where my hands would be while playing. Out of the black box two rods projected like antenna. Each ended in a black eye the size of a pencil eraser.

"This is the way this works, Mr. Scottman," Sam said, and the gadget clattered down between the pedals onto the floor. It took a while to fish it out and put back in place. Sam bent a paperclip from the shelf beside my pencils to make a bracket that slid into the crack at the front of the keys to secure it before he had to chase it again.

"For my friends in the string section, I made this switch work with a toe toggle on the foot of their music stand. Tip it one way, pages advance; tip the other way, pages go back, one page per tap. For you, I made a light sensor. Flip your finger in front of this one, pages advance and that one for back. Try it."

The work I was on jumped forward with a flick of my finger. When I moved my hand to turn the page back, the page jumped forward one more before going back.

"Let me change the angle of the sensors."

In a minute, I could flip easily through music with no trouble.

"I put on a button so you can switch it on and off with one hand. Just press it down."

I did and the red eye inside it winked out.

"It runs on a disc battery." He removed the gadget from its paperclip bracket and showed how the back slid off with one-handed thumb pressure. The silver disc popped up on one edge so I could grab it. I put it back in and slid the closing into place. "It wirelessly talks to your computer," Sam continued.

I held it out to him with raised eyebrows.

"This one is a pilot project. I don't know how well it will work, long term, so you get it for free if you tell me how well or badly it works."

Neither knew of my resident page turner but I wasn't going to discourage such enthusiastic effort directed my way. Besides, I'd have it if he was sick or moved away. I'd keep it with the metronome.

I thanked Sam with a hand over my heart and a prayerful hand-raise and suggested with a wave, that we have tea. The cart was clattering towards the sitting room.

"I also bring a progress report on the digitizing project," Margaret said as we took our seats with her full cups. I noticed the store-bought cookies in the tin box. Brad calls them flint and steel. Margaret noticed my disparaging glance and pointed to the table in our corner where a whole biscuit box of her cookies lay waiting.
A parchment divider separated the gingerbread cookies from the oatmeal chocolate chip ones. They were stacked up at least three deep on each side of the divider.

"We're on target for completion," she announced.

I signaled a cheer.

I saw Brad come in over her shoulder. His hair was still plastered down from the pool. He had his tea on his walker. My wave distracted him from his glare at the cookies. He lit up like a sign when he saw us; he didn't even sit down before he'd loaded a gingerbread couple onto his saucer.

"Fred and Ginger," he explained and then sat down in our circle.

Margaret had to explain to Sam, the reference to the dance team of a distant day, whose music was part of the library she was working on.

"Getting back to the project," she said. "I've taken it upon myself to augment the book material I'm digitizing. I've added copies of the index of each book. You had marked entries in many books. You can't access those pages from the Index copy, but you would at least know what book to look up on-line, or from a library, to get the material you needed. It has taken longer to do each book, but I thought it was the right thing to do."

I nodded enthusiastically.

"The only way to access those Index entries would be to retype the whole book. We'd have to expand the spread sheet we set up to such a size that it would be unusable. That just can't happen."

I gave an *OK* shrug.

"Since the university declined the collection, have you thought about offering the stuff on-line?"

I shook my head.

"If the university isn't interested, maybe someone out in the great ether would like the collection or a piece of it."

I shoveled a hand toward her hoping I was suggesting she should go ahead and spread the word.

"You want me to advertise it?"

I nodded enthusiastically.

"Have you thought about doing the bakery business and selling on-line," Brad asked looking wistfully at his empty saucer. "You might deliver your delicacies by bicycle courier all over town."

He was sniffing the air expectantly.

Margaret was reaching for the box to offer him another cookie when I stopped her hand. She looked at me and I demonstrated how overwhelming and tearful Brad's performance had been, then waved Brad's con away. She got it. Brad got no more cookies.

Our visit ended with the student's need to return to other duties. We waved goodbye through the window as they left.

"What was Sam here for? Are they an item?"

I shrugged, then beckoned Brad back to the organ in the Dining Room; I'd left my whiteboard there. On it I scribbled, *you can be replaced*, and I held up the gadget.

Brad examined it then suddenly, in a sleight of hand pretended to drop it on the floor and stamp on it. He caught me completely by surprise. I stared at him open-mouthed.

He smiled and held up the gadget he hadn't dropped at all and put out his other hand.

"Ransom time," he declared nodding to the box under my arm.

With as much dignity as I could muster, I surrendered the box for the page turner. Brad took out two chocolate chip cookies and handed it back smiling.

16
GIFTING

The students delivered the hard drive, and backup of my music library at Easter before they got into exams. It was marvelous. I could call up any of my music in a fraction of the time I'd had to spend digging it out of boxes. Jess had the foundation for a master's thesis, she said, and would be writing it during her next year. I presented cheques they were not expecting on top of the boarding arrangements we'd agreed to.

A host of requests for old music came from Margaret's on-line efforts. She marketed them at a dollar each if the purchaser picked it up or extra to be mailed. I was astonished at what she raised in the sale.
I told her to share it with the others. I could also do the arithmetic on what she sold and what didn't. I didn't ask where or when the rest disappeared. I can't look at a cardboard box without wondering if one of my Handel

Oratorios or Mozart's F minor Fantasy is in there. What an insult to shred such stuff to carry anything as mundane as candy bars or cornflakes. I frequently look up at their pictures in the poster on my wall and ask forgiveness before I wave a memory stick that holds everything they ever wrote and think *but I saved you here.*

Jessica said the Index will be part of her Appendix to her thesis so it will vanish into some electronic world that is good until the lights go out, I guess. In my experience, nothing outlasts paper. Look what happened to the Ten Commandments; see anyone reading a stone tablet lately? So, the loss of the paper copies grieves me.

When I get down that low, I try to imagine who bought those copies of music that moved millions.

Are they inspiring a novice as they did me? Are they gathering dust on a collector's shelf waiting to be exploited by someone who couldn't tell a toccata from a teacup? It is the way to hope for me. I can't imagine a depressing possibility for things, without imagining an inspiring one. Pollyanna is my name when it is not Don Quixote de la Mancha.

With the end of the school year, the students were set to move out, back home to jobs they had arranged. Could I send some of the ghosts of generations past with them? I asked the bus driver to drop me off at my house on the way home from church.

"Will I be able to rent a room here next Fall?" asked Jessica.

Margaret was trekking boxes to Sam's car in the driveway.

Not unless the Real Estate market goes to pot. It is time for me to cut the cord, or is it chord, if I can use that phrase. The kids want me to sell as well so they don't have to do the maintenance that falls on their shoulders.

That's what I wanted to say. Those are the words that
went through my head and I opened my mouth to say
them and then stopped before I embarrassed myself. I
shook my head. On her way back in from the car, I
stopped Margaret and beckoned her, with Jessica, into
the Dining Room. I tried to indicate I was looking for
Trudy by looking past them.

"Trudy is at work. She's finishing her last shift at
the coffee shop."

I pulled open the china cabinet door, the drawers, and
cupboards. I got the feeling they were dreading the next
moment. I stood aside and waved to them to take what
they wanted.

There was a chorus of "Oh No's," and "I can't's."
"Your kids should have these," was the next protest. I
had to silence them with upraised hands.

I set my whiteboard on the table and wrote, *kids took
what they wanted. Can't use/take these.* I showed them

and wiped it clean then wrote anew. *Wonderful thing you did for me and them*. I pointed to the wall in the next room decorated now with rows of holes and empty picture hooks. *Hope you will remember. Please take.*

I turned to lift out the bags in which other family candelabras hid and gave one to each girl, then reached back for their mates. These were not the Christmas dinner ones, but the relics of other families whose story has been lost. I think both girls were looking at each other behind my back wondering what to do.

"Are you sure? These have many memories for you." Margaret said.

I shook my head and wrote that these are different from the ones they had seen earlier.

"Then I would be honoured to take these and remember your generosity and those guys," Margaret said as she hooked her thumb to the wall behind her.

She took the matching candlestick in its bag from me. Jessica did the same, but she had a tear in her eye. With both their hands loaded, I turned and pulled out the linen tablecloths from the long drawer in the bureau and draped one over each bundle. I tried to mime they were to wrap and pad the candlesticks with them.

I don't think they knew what to do. I was beginning to panic that they would back away before I could finish the moment. I put the last pair of candlesticks on the table and pointed that they were for Trudy, with the last two linen tablecloths.

They both nodded in understanding and were shuffling to leave when I pulled out the Royal Worcester cake plate and gave it to Margaret and signaled it was for cookies.

"You want me to bring you more cookies?" she interpreted.

I shook my head and pointed to her.

"Well I agree, any cookies or squares would look good on that." She accepted the gift graciously then held up her hand to stop me.

I got Jessica to accept the pair of Royal Worcester teacups. I set the pair of Belleek candy dishes with Trudy's candlesticks. I noticed she always had a bowl of almonds around wherever she was working. Both were in the hallway almost out the door when I remembered.

I sighed then *Hmmmm'd* as loudly as I could to turn them back.
 I reached to the back of the china cabinet as they were protesting anew but they stopped as soon as I pulled out more candle snuffers I remembered were there. They each took one and we all laughed. In that moment I was sure the story would pass to any who lit the candles. Duty done.

17
THE ANTIQUE DEALER

The antique dealer came by appointment to survey the furniture. Both the kids were with me when he came.

"So he doesn't take advantage of you," Jean explained.

Donald answered the door. I sat in the armed chair that hadn't made it back to the Dining Room where it had been holding paper in my old music room.

The man was scruffily dressed. As Donald spoke to him in the hall, I noticed his eyes darting about.

"Oh, they don't make them like that anymore," he said when he got to the Dining Room suite.

He'd walked past me as though I wasn't there.

I guess I'm not an old enough antique, I thought.

"The leaves to extend it are behind the cabinet," Jean said.

He ignored the comment.

"The problem is that few people have a room big enough to take this thing," the dealer said dismissively. "I'll bet it would extend out into the street." Somehow, he said it as though we should be ashamed to admit it.

The cabinet that had had the candlesticks in it, stared empty-eyed from the corner. He tried the latch and made some sort of decision. He pointed at the bottom shelf.

"The dishes are of no value anymore," the dealer said. All that gold leaf decoration … really out of style now."
He didn't mention that he had an agent who recovered the gold and at over a thousand dollars an ounce, it was worth it. He simply smashed the dishes and dumped them into a processor that removed the gold. The gold in the set might net close to that.

"My G… . How many pieces do you have there?"

Jean recited the inventory. I watched his eyes as he flicked from one thing to another. He wasn't looking at the dishes; he looked too long at the cabinets.

"Well If we agree on the furniture, I'll take these away for you. Save you a trip and hassle at the dump. A fine set in its day, but not now," the dealer said. "Any more?"

Jean called his attention to the display of fancy teacups.

"A buck apiece if I can sell them at all," he said with a dismissive wave. "Anything else?"

I remembered the time that went into selecting similar ones for gifts when we were young, the considerations of what else the recipient had, the cost of this one, how you could see the shadow of your finger through the side to tell you it was fine porcelain. Each giver took that same care to present these, and he said they were hardly worth his time to pick up. *Rude,* I thought

"There is a couch that's hardly been used since it was reupholstered," Jean continued, "and a matching Queen Anne chair. Side tables and an antique pair of chairs in the Living Room. There are dressers and beds upstairs."

The dealer thumped into the next room and up the stairs behind the kids with hardly a pause. I could hear the sparse exchanges. I knew from the sounds which carved bedstead they were looking at with its spindled footboard, and ornamental head.

As the conversation droned away, I found myself daydreaming; I couldn't help but think back to that day long ago when my wife and I had gone to one of those travelling antique evaluation shows. They fill time on TV with giddy people being told that the heirloom that they had been using for a doorstop was worth more than their house. The film footage for such events is found in places like we were going to. Here I sat looking out the window past the blank walls as though the movie of that distant day was going on before me.

Marie had long wondered at the value of a throw rug that had been in her mother's house as long as Marie could remember. It was under her rocking chair in the Living Room where she sat when she did all her knitting. It had to be antique. And it never seemed to wear; the colours were still those she recalled. There were no worn places despite its age. It had to have been made really well to have stood up so well for so long - well that and being properly cared for over the years.

Marie remembered as a child, taking it to the clothesline and beating it with the tool of looped steel that hid at the back of the cleaning closet for just that purpose. Her young arms ached after the task which ended when no more dust fell from the rug. Mother always complimented her on the job and on how bright the colours were now that half a year's dust and grit had been pounded out of it. She had to put it back a quarter turn from what it had been when she lifted it, *so that the wear was distributed*, her mother had said.

"I really want to find out how much it is worth," Marie had insisted.

She'd bought the tickets and paid her appraisal fee. I had agreed to accompany her, but it had to be an early appointment because I had a wedding to play for that afternoon. I wanted to be out of the place before lunch. As the day in question approached, we got a notification that because of the popular demand, the opening time would be half an hour earlier.

"So, there will be a line to get into the hall, and then a lineup at the appraiser's table," I deduced. "We'd better be out early so we don't get caught." Marie was not amused when the bedside alarm went off and it was still dark. She took her coffee in a travel mug instead of dallying with it over the morning newspaper.

We arrived at the parking area before staff had placed the signs. Marie deduced the proper doorway into the hall so that an hour before opening time, we were first in line standing across from a row of tables where volunteers were being trained on how to find a visitor's name, which coloured wrist band to attach to the person and which colour-coded ticket to give the person to match the time of their appointment with an appraiser.

Marie had her rug rolled and standing at attention in a bundle buggy when we began our wait. She took her coat off and used the carpet as a hall tree. She pulled out her coffee mug and leaned against the wall to relax in preparation for the coming excitement.

I turned to the next in line to ask how she had heard about the event. I got the fifteen-minute life-story ending with the secretive removal of a battered blue velvet box from her purse and a body-shielded peek at the cameo pendant inside that had been her grandmother's in the old country.

The organizer noticed the lineup was now out the door. A crackling conversation from the radio on her belt said the parking lot was full. She announced that there were four desks at which we could register so could we please move into four lines and let more people into the building.

I recall being thumped by a painting held by a serious looking senior.

"Sorry," he apologized, and he took a place behind us. The cameo lady was now at the head of a line in the middle of the hall.

The man with the painting set the it against the wall and stretched sore muscles. Everyone was tired from standing.

"I hope it is valuable," I said nodding at the frame wrapped in an old flannel sheet inside a clear plastic garbage bag.

"Oh, I'm sure it is," said his wife. She pulled the corner of the sheet aside a smidgen so that a part signature was visible. "He used to be our neighbour in Toronto," she explained. "He's very well known. My parents each bought the other this painting and then it came to us. We have three children, and each has fallen in love with it," she gushed.

"That sounds like a problem in the making," I had suggested. "Have you decided who will get it … later?"

The man grimaced.

The lady twisted her hands, "We thought we should get it evaluated, as part of our estate planning."

"There is a dealer in Dundas," I said, "who will digitally photograph that painting and make a print you couldn't tell from the original. He did it for an old picture of my mother and fixed the tear as well. It looks the way it did when she was a child - almost a century ago now."

While the man brightened at the thought and asked me again for the name of the dealer, his wife was dwelling on the antagonism that such a plan would create - giving two children a fake.

"Well how would they feel?" she asked.

The supervising lady released the lines at that point. People struggled to hoist heavy boxes and awkward cylinders. We met new participants at the lineup to the hall within which the experts were seated at their tables.

We were given a floor plan and the specialties of the appraisers. Marie identified the professional most likely to evaluate her treasure.

"Through the door and to the right," she said. "Table number six."

"Doors open in ten minutes," said the security guard.

Our new line-mate had an ornately carved walking cane. He showed me the date of *1884* cut into the stub of a branch.

"I'd like to know where it came from. I'm trying to trace the ancestry of the person who brought it into our family."

"It certainly is a handsome piece," I observed. "What is it made of?"

"It's Rowanwood," he replied and then went on to tell of the wood's mystic properties and the mythic figures also shown in the carving. The man's knowledge was effusive. "You see it grew with this side exposed and this side protected," he said and pointed to scars and trimmed twigs.

"You can go in now," said the guard pulling open one of the double doors while an assistant opened the other.

We made a beeline for Table six, Marie stepping quickly, the buggy clattering behind her. I watched people enter, stop inside about four steps from the door and gape around till a companion figured out the layout.

I caught up to Marie as she was asking if she should lay out the carpet. She'd flicked off her coat that had covered it, like a magician. The expert leaned across the table and folded back a corner.

"Well," he said kindly, "tell me about it." He sat down and gestured us to the chairs for visitors. The carpet stood mutely in its buggy between us, awaiting sentence. Marie launched into her story.

I noticed how intently the man watched her, attentive to every detail.

Marie was finishing the tale when the evaluator said, "I can see your mother bought well. That it has survived in its current condition is a testament to the love and care that must have filled the house. She was also a very frugal woman, I suspect. This carpet is not an antique, by most standards. It is machine made, probably in postwar Belgium. She would be proud to know it had been so well cared for by her child."

Marie began to realize the gentle rebuke of her dream. A silence fell on the table despite the clatter and conversation nearby.

"Is it valuable?" she asked tentatively.

"I think it's value is in the memories it carries like the colours dyed into it," the man said. "To anyone else, it might be worth fifty dollars."

Marie was momentarily stunned but then burst out laughing. The emotional tension that had led to the moment came to a crashing stop.

"Fifty bucks," she finally said though the laughter.

"About that."

"Well you've given me a new window on my mother," Marie said as she jumped from her chair looking like the weight of the world had been lifted from her shoulders. We turned to go.

The room behind us was jammed with people all clutching their boxes and wrapped treasures.

I could see the man with the cane also heading for the door.

"He said five hundred to get us away from the table," the man said. "He really doesn't have a clue. Thought it might be plastic at one point. Suggested it was carved on the boat that brought him over. I don't think he knows much about sailing and trying to carve on a boat bouncing about."

*

The memories floated through my head as I heard the voices upstairs walk across the fifty-dollar carpet that was beside the bed, and back into the hall.

"I'll bet that weighs a ton," I heard when they got to the ornate Victorian dresser and dressing table with mirror in the guest bedroom. "You should rent this place out as a movie set." He was trying to be funny, but I could tell from the looks on the kids as they came down, that they were feeling badly about the experience.

Back in the hallway, the Dealer went through some head shaking as he looked back into the Dining Room. He waved a hand expansively.

"Nine hundred for the lot," he said as though he was doing us a favour.

The kids looked at each other and then me. I shook my head.

"That's your best offer?" Donald asked.

"That's as far as I can go. I've got my van in the driveway, I can take it off your hands right now." He pulled a wad of bills from his pocket and peeled off some bills.

"Have you got a card?" Jean asked. "I think we need to talk it over."

"Ma'am, you won't get a better offer anywhere and you'll be done."

"Maybe we can call you if we have a card?" Jean insisted.

The man made a show of contained exasperation as he put his money away and pulled a business card from a shirt pocket. He handed the card over and pulled the door open muttering under his breath.

"Bye, and thank you," Donald called after him.

Donald closed the door, "Boy, that was a downer!" and then he went into chapter and verse about how the dealer had denigrated everything they showed him.

He was drawing a fresh breath when there was a knock at the door.

"Hello," said the man in clean jeans and a work shirt on the porch. "You asked me to come by and look at some antiques. I think you said you were downsizing."

Jean jumped forward, "Yes. You were talking to me. My goodness, I lost track of time."

"Well, I think I'm a little early, Ma'am. Was that my competitor I saw driving back down the street?"

"We thought we needed a couple of estimates. We've never done this before."

"Perfectly correct, Ma'am."

I was introduced and my speechlessness explained and that the house was being cleared out because of my move. I noticed how he watched the person he was speaking to.

"If there is anything, I can help you with, I'd be pleased to offer my suggestions." He pulled a business card from a leather case like a binder, "Here's my card."

Hiram Weaver was the name on the card.

"Let's start in the Dining Room," my daughter suggested and led the way through my old Music Room towards double sliding doors that stood open. I joined the parade.

Hiram stepped to the down side of the table to catch the light shining off it.   He moved along the length.

"I can see you have really looked after this piece for probably fifty years." He stepped back to look at the carved legs and nodded. "More, I'd say." I think that was built in the early nineteen hundreds.

I nodded.

"Are there leaves to extend the table?

"Four. Behind the cupboard."

"Could I look at them?

Again, he examined each carefully. He quickly eyed them for warping as he put them back making sure they did not rub against each other.

"Those chairs in the other room belong to this table?" he asked to confirm.

I nodded. He went back to look at each chair. leaned on the back to check for loose joints and sat in a couple.

"You've replaced the leather on the seats. Did you replace the padding below?"

"It was pretty flat," Jean interjected.

"Well this table is really four, in my store," he said. "Apartments and condos don't take stuff like this easily - too big. I would cut it apart and use the ends of the table for two separate tables, and make two more, each with a drop leaf, from the leaves. I can easily sell the tables for about two hundred each because they are of solid wood not particleboard. To do that, I couldn't offer you more than four hundred for the tables and chairs. The chairs need re-gluing and some loving care to refinish the backs, but they sit comfortably and would be a good purchase for anyone. I like that you have two armchairs."

He wrote the amount in a column beside the description and then photographed the items.

It went on like that for the rest of the afternoon.

"This is what we do with fancy teacups," he said as he called up on his iPad.

A collection of wall sconces and light fixtures that had incorporated old cups and saucers. He explained how he could repair the veneer on a headboard, or dresser, how it was better not to strip off the finish because of the provenance it bestowed.

When we stood in the hallway again, he handed a copy of the list he had made with the price he would pay.

"Do you still have my card," he asked again.

I held up a hand and did an eye contact with each child. Everyone agreed. The total he was offering was about the same as the other guy, but this man cared. The other was just flipping stuff. We didn't like that attitude.

Hiram caught the silent signals we exchanged.

"I know it is hard to part with stuff that has been such an important part of your life for so long."

"Every item has a memory and people sometimes worry that the chain will be lost if any of the links

212

disappear. But from my experience, there is not one person I've dealt with that doesn't say two weeks later, that they should have done it years ago. Those memory chains were getting pretty heavy to look after. Though you feel stressed now, you are sending these pieces on to new owners who will treasure them as you have. You can feel confident you have seen these pieces to a safe home."

That did it.

"We'd be pleased to have you take everything," said Jean. "I think my Dad feels it is like a legacy that he is leaving to others and you are the person who can get it to those others who will treasure these pieces."

Everyone turned to me. I nodded around a tear.

"We include a story with each item we sell," Hiram said.

He continued, "So when you sign the contract for us to take the listed items at the price stated, there is a clause that says we can include what you tell us. We don't or can't always use Auntie's name, but we can say where it came from, what its value was originally, how it came into a family, that sort of thing. Not everyone wants to know or buy stuff that will last a lifetime, but we have more business than we can handle now because enough people do want to know."

"Would you like to sign the contract now Dad?" Jean asked.

I scrawled my signature with a smile.

"Let me call my team with the truck," Hiram said as he stepped out onto the porch.

"I'll take you back," Jean said to me. "Donald can wait and lock up."

I patted both my kids on the back and headed for the car.

Wish I could tell the others, I thought.

18
THE PROPOSAL

"Your house sold quickly," Brad said as he joined me at breakfast.

I handed him the card that was still in my pocket; under Hiram's name was, *Memories Recycled.*

"He took your stuff then?"

I nodded and pulled up a picture on my iPad of the dining room table and wrote out what Hiram said he would do with the table. It took a while to mime and write how the table would be treated. *Wanted story too*, I scribbled on my whiteboard.

"Well you did your duty, eh? New use found for good things; story preserved. How good is that?"

I gave him a thumbs-up salute.

"What's the paper?"

I pushed it across to him and he read it as he ate his porridge. I got a coffee refill.

"So, you think there should be some music students living in here? You know there aren't enough spaces for the seniors who need them don't you. Why would this place bring in a couple university kids?

Quality of life, I scribbled then wiped it and wrote, *Ours! We need to feel we have a place where we belong. Music can be that place when all else is gone.*

"What's that say?" Brad asked where I ran out of room and I rewrote my last sentence.

I took back the board to write, *need place and time to share talent.*

"You're talking about the monotones here."

I shook my head in disagreement then wrote, *stories.*

"You aren't planning to bring in a Nursery School also by chance?"

I pointed to the page he hadn't gotten to, where that topic was listed as the second reason for the letter to the Business Administrator.

"I'm going to move out!"

I touched his hand and shook my head energetically. By hand waving I tried to show I thought he had many stories to tell that others should hear along with my pleading glance.

"OK, since you put it that way, I'll stay," he said mischievously.

I really should not let him jerk my chain that way.

He set the letter to our Administrator aside and looked back at the other pages that were crossways to the first ones.

"What's that?"

I handed over what I had sent to the Church Secretary to include in the Order of Service for two weeks ahead along with the selections I would play at the parts of the service where they were expected.

Each selection had its own heading- Prelude, Offertory, Postlude.

It was the three long paragraphs of description of the things to listen for, that flowed onto the next page that raised his eyebrows.

I watched as Brad's eyes swept through my description of the Prelude meant to put the congregation in a prayerful mood, but they stopped on the Offertory. He raised an eye on the Offertory Anthem.

"What is that?" he demanded, pointing to my title.

I raised my eyebrows in feigned wonder.

"A baroque fantasy of a theme by J. Gorne, 1932. The melody is based on a Russian-Jewish lullaby sung to the composer by his mother," Brad read the first sentence. "This looks suspicious to me."

I beckoned him to the organ in the corner where I opened the roll-up and handed him earphones. I settled myself.

I don't need to call up music; I knew this one really well and I could improvise all over the place and extend as long as it takes for the ushers to gather at the back.

When I see, in my mirror, they are ready to bring the Offering plates forward, I raise the key and open up with the majestic chords everyone expects to accompany their gift-giving. I started off in a contemplative minor key on the flute and gradually added the other voices as I meandered through the melody.

As soon as Brad figured out the theme, he burst out laughing and waved his hand to keep me going into one variation after another. Then I went into the magnificent March of the Loaded Ushers that brings everyone to their feet.

"How do you get away with that?" he asked when I lifted my hands from the final chord.

Only a few of my friends, those I've taught to listen, recognize it. I knew my lessons were successful when I tried that out the first time, I thought.

"What's all the commotion?" asked the Business Administrator as she came around the partition.

I had to play it again for her.

"Do you recognize the theme?" Brad said.

She shrugged.

"It is one of the most famous themes of the Depression. It's called **Brother can you spare a dime,** and he plays it in a churchy disguise while they take up the Offering. Don't you think that is funny?"

She smiled politely, but still didn't know the context of the music so missed the point.

She was also getting used to anything connected with Scottman being off any track she learned about at University.

"Well try this," Brad said. "It's Gerald's suggestion that we bring in university music students and nursery school kids to make we seniors feel useful."

"Did you write this?" she asked me.

I nodded.

Her look said *I might have guessed.* She thought back to the crowded halls outside his room. *It all started with letting that organ come in here,* she thought again. But she pasted on a neutral face as she read further down the proposal.

"You know I've heard of this elsewhere."

I held my hand out in supplication.

"Let me take it up the line." She was scanning the highlights I'd bulleted at the bottom. "It might mean we need to increase the rates of the others."

I shook my head and pointed to the rates the students would pay.

I mimed pushing a rock.

"OK. I'll take it further."

She couldn't wait to point out to her superior that this is entirely what she foretold. While the chance to put in a dig was too good to miss, she'd rescue him with the article from a recent journal that reported a Care facility in the States doing exactly this, with beneficial results to the residents.

She had turned away with my paper leaving me with my material for the Church. Brad waived to it.

"How big is the Order of Service? Don't you think this is a little long?"

I shook my head.

"I'll bet that secretary does. I'll bet it pushes a single page folded, to at least an insert. I'll bet this is almost as long as the minister's sermon and she doesn't have to print that."

I said nothing, just sighed. *More stuff I didn't know what to do with,* I thought.

I gave the paper to Brad pointing to the Postlude.

"A melody based on a folk theme by Harvey and Pearl encouraging shared family entertainment in the post-war period," he read.

"Now I am more than suspicious," he said.

I flipped the organ to the speakers and entered into the bouncy melody in three-four time.

When I got to the chorus, he burst out with the words our generation all knew, "Don't play Bingo tonight, Mother. Stay home with Father and me."

Late diners picked it up on the other side of the partition. I continued through the verse decorated with a lot of magisterial sound and tempo which threw everyone off. But when we got to the chorus again, more voices joined in.

"And nobody at church knows this?" Brad asked in amazement.

I shrugged and shut things down. *We don't have Bingo at our church*, I wanted to say. But I couldn't.

19
INSPIRATION

Is it because we don't have stuff anymore that we feel so
lost in a place like this? I ask myself this all the time.
When we give up those memory chains Hiram spoke of,
do we lose the anchor they connected us to? I don't think
I feel it as keenly as some others here. I have my organ
and wall of memories for refuge when I feel unable to
bear the loneliness of others about me as well as my own.
It is the time between concerts, like now, when I find
myself most strongly in retreat. At the concerts,
everybody sings along, and the room takes on a shine that
outdoes the chandeliers. Take, for instance, two weeks
ago; you'd think we'd found the elixir of youth.

The choir was singing *Take me out to the Ball game* far too hard to stay on tune, but do they care? They're all smiling and singing then burst into laughing when the staff asks where that song came from.

They say rats in cages make up games to play. We'd organized a watching of a World Series Games after we got the Kitchen Staff to make something approaching Cracker Jack by spraying popcorn with a thin butterscotch syrup loaded up in a window spray bottle and then running the creation back through the oven to harden it up. The staff stopped making that stuff after the first game because there were so many denture issues. And the nurses gave the diabetics grief. With restrictions on snacks there wasn't such a communal watching of the rest of the series; things seemed to go flat.

Then it was this week's concert. I featured Thanksgiving hymns which many could sing from memory.

Over tea I heard people sharing times of being on a farm or looking at the rows of preserves in their cold cellars. But the feelings seemed to vanish with the echoes.

Maybe that's a slight exaggeration. I am stopped all the time by others who tell me how much they enjoyed the last singsong. Staff tell me again and again that those in the memory suites show distinct improvement whenever they get a chance to join in the group sings. But those compliments come as I walk an institutional hall through a haze of floral perfume that never defiled my home space.

The only place I have as an escape space is either behind the partitions at my organ, or with the composers in my bedroom. The Nevermore Retirement Home aims to preserve the body, but not the brain; I find sanctuary through withdrawal into my memory world rather than walking this real one.

Brad knocked on the door and broke my mood.

"Margaret and Sam are doing a pub crawl and asked if we'd come. I said yes, so get your coat."

Margaret and Jessica had responded to the invitation for music students to take up residence in the Do I Care Retirement Home after my effort back in the Spring. They share a suite and augment the weekend concert after lunch on Saturdays with either something they play or that one of their friends brings in as part of their performance training.

I manage to get them each to teach how to hear a single element they perform. It tickles me down to my keys when I hear how it gives everyone something to talk about and listen for next time. But Brad immediately revealed another benefit of their presence when I tried to shrug him off.

I was going to practice, I tried to say by turning back to my keyboard.

"Practice at the Pub. They've got a piano there. Come on. They won't wait forever."

Reluctantly I stood and snagged my coat off the hook inside the closet.

"Not that way," Brad said as I made to turn towards the main entrance. The nursing station was that way also.

He steered me in the opposite direction and out the fire escape into the parking lot where Sam's car was running, and the headlights were on.

"Two hours till bed check," announced Brad as he snapped on his seatbelt beside me in the back seat.

"Watches set," Sam said from the front. I could see the glow from a cell phone lighting up Margaret's face as she pecked something into it.

When we got there, the place was crowded with members of a Welsh Male Choir who were enjoying an afterglow following a concert nearby. Margaret had found out about this and who was in charge. They must have a marshal who lines them up at concert and checked they were in uniform. He was in charge in the Pub because the conductor tried to avoid these things.

"He doesn't like the songs we sing when we're out of his control and he's embarrassed at how well we sing without him leading," explained the red-faced man with a stein in his hand. All around laughed heartily.

Brad explained I was an organist and before he seemed to finish, I found a pint in my hand and myself in front of a scarred upright grand, hemmed in by forty cheering faces.

"*Cwm Rhondda*," said the marshal in my ear.

I set my mug at the end of the keyboard and hit the chords of the last bars that are often used as an introduction. To my surprise they did not sing *"Guide me Oh thou Great Jehovah."* The words they were using were to *"Clementine."*

"Oh my darlin', Oh my darlin, Oh my darlin' Clementine," they boomed, in perfect four-part harmony.

I just kept going. I can't recall all the words, but they ended with something rude about how Clementine was missed until they met her sister.

"There's a Long Long Trail," shouted a voice from the back and I hit the intro. Bam, they came in with a wall of sound.

"Streets of London. Colin, come up here," called a voice about two swallows after that song ended.

A bearded smiling face sang the solo line and the choir snuck in so softly on the chorus you hardly heard them as they swelled to, *"And say for you that the sun don't shine."*

233

Tenors improvised an obligato.

"Roll out the Barrel," cried someone to hustle off the cheers for Colin and it went on like that for over an hour.

If I didn't know the melody they just asked for a chord. Sometimes I could just follow along, but I couldn't follow them when they got to *White Rose*. It wasn't in my repertoire, but they all knew it. I just remember two lines from the chorus:

I love the White Rose in its splendour, I love the White Rose in its bloom … and the tenors that made me tingle.

These guys sang thirty pub songs for memory, all in harmony, before Brad tapped me on the shoulder and pointed to Margaret and Sam at the door. They were singing a cappella as we left.

All I could do is mouth the word, *WOW*! as we walked to the car. I gave a thumbs up salute and big smile to Margaret when she looked my way.

From the Parking Lot, Brad guided me to the fire escape again, where he had wedged the door open with a stick. We entered and were both in our rooms when Eva made her rounds. I was just getting undressed.

"What's that smell?" she asked. "Have you got beer in here?"

I just shrugged and looked innocent, but I think she is suspicious that age and deception might have overcome youth and skill.

20
NOT ANOTHER ONE

The Pub event with the male choir made me realize
something important, I think. I wonder if I've traded my
old material world stuff for the mental stuff of
experience. Brad articulated it for me over breakfast the
next morning.

"Dodged a bullet last night, did we?" he asked as
he spread jam on his toast.

I nodded, "My faithful Ms. Eva said I smelled like
a brewery. I suggested the ventilation system had
backfired. But I did have to get up a lot during the night
for many pees. Well worth it though, would you agree?"

Another nod.

"You really impressed me the way you could play all those songs they kept bringing up. How do you know all those?"

I waved a hand in the air as though they were hanging is space all about us. How could I explain that musical notes are all connected by rules and that if you know a few, and enough rules, you can accompany people who are on a predictable path.

"I have new appreciation for your musical skills," Brad complimented with the lift of a jammy crust. "We should do that again."

I nodded enthusiastically then I pointed towards the distant pub and beckoned.

"You think they should come here?" Brad exploded in laughter. "Now that would get the Administrator in a knot eh?"

I pointed to the partitions behind which my organ slept.

"Well I'll give you that. You do have the instrument to accompany them. Maybe we should form a committee to study the feasibility."

I rolled my eyes but resolved to see if Margaret could bring their leader over to assess the place.

*

My resolve was tested sorely. My typing skill was definitely not up to the task, but it was the only way by which I could communicate the proposal. I had managed to get students into the place and that was an encouraging success.

But that happened over a single conversation that grew elsewhere in spite of me. Bringing in a large group of men to practice and rehearse was going to be a logarithmic jump.

Fortunately, Brad was dissuaded from organizing a Committee. Margaret, he, and I formed what Margaret called a 'Brainstorming Group.' Well I sure felt stormed by the time our first meeting ended. It was only Margaret's gingerbread cookies that made it tolerable and we polished off the boxful that she brought.

"A Committee will be appropriate to seek resident input once the big picture has been sketched out," Margaret explained. "If this is going to fly, you get a big picture, and then you seek the help of people here to implement the parts of it."

That was not the way my life had been. The Priest or Minister decided and went ahead. Sometimes I was told the plan; mostly not. And I would make up my music program no matter what he or she did, but hoped I was supplementing his or her efforts in ways they didn't know about.

"The other thing that is involved is you are moving in on what people call their home," Margaret cautioned.

239

"There are seventy-five seniors here who call this home. You can't make a decision that demands they suddenly share their space with a bunch of strangers."

Well that was her view. It was not mine, nor was it the view of several who had told me their feelings. Others had forgotten what a home had been and accepted that this was the price of finding someone to look after them; this was as good as it was going to get.

"This is a warehouse," I protested, "a comfortable resort we'd like to leave if we could only find a way to do so. Where is the way back to all the stuff that made us feel at home?"

"The things with the tarnish that each piece had developed from both use and neglect, but which marked the space we had made for ourselves. I spend all my time trying to put myself somewhere else, like the church, like my music room practicing, like my library preparing material for anyone who will read or listen."

When I was finally able to convey that thought, Margaret re-articulated the objective, "You don't want to invite a male choir, you want your home back."

Click, I responded, and threw up my hand in joy. Somebody finally figured it out!

"And the choir is just a manifestation of having the power you used to enjoy at home?"

Click.

"Does this ring a bell with you, Brad?" she asked.

"At home we used to have wine with our evening meal," Brad said. "I'd go to the wine closet to select a bottle from the many batches we'd made together, and which were aging there, and bring it back. I'd hope I put the corkscrew back in the drawer with the string last time and would be delighted to find it there. I had a corkscrew that, once twisted into the cork, engaged a different thread so by turning another part, the cork came out

241

easily; we bought it at a flea market in Paris. I never did that without thinking of those times and how wonderful it was to re-enact them.

He took a deep breath and continued, "When I moved here, all of that disappeared. I put on a brave face, packed two suitcases, and left. What do you need a corkscrew for in a Retirement Home? You can't get a drink here without a prescription and there is probably a labour code or liability coverage needed to permit me to open a bottle of wine at the table. So, do I live here? No! No! and NO! I reside here."

Margaret was knocked back into her chair by the substance and strength with which Brad presented his case.

"Does the Business Administrator know how you feel?" she asked.

"Your point being?"

"If they knew, they might try to accommodate your desires."

"There's a reason we call this place, "Nevercare," or like derogatives. Everyone gets meals on time, a comfortable bed, and medicine to keep us alive forever. So, our expletives are not really accurate. The staff and owners cater to what they think care means, but their care and concern is not living - only life. What Gerald has brought into this place is a glimmer of what is beyond survival, with all the music he does. He started a choir that by most standards is probably terrible, but it is ours and we love him for it. By wanting to bring in another choir, he is only pushing the same rock up the same hill."

He paused, but only for a second, "If I were going to broaden his theme, I'd have us making our own wine and beer and have pub nights like the program director offers Bingo or Euchre. We'd have a local Probis chapter to being in speakers, and scheduled trips to the Theatre for movies, plays, operas, and I'd send in decorators to renovate every room to suit those who inhabit it rather than force them into the institutional mould they had to accept to get in here."

Margaret was astounded.

"And I've worked myself up to such a state, I need some Nitro so I'll go find the nurse before I expire here on the floor."

He stood abruptly, whirled his walker into position, and stalked off towards the hall.

We both watched as he turned the corner headed towards the nursing station before Margaret asked me, "Are there many who think like that?"

I held up a hand and waggled it.

"So some, maybe not a lot, but a frustrated few at least."

Click.

While Brad had been talking, I'd pecked out on my iPad some points I now handed over to Margaret.

CHOIR THOUGHTS

- Is there enough parking?
- Were the washrooms adequate?
- Why not have a mixed choir?
- Would a women's choir get the same treatment if they wanted to come on another night?
- What about the residents who used the dining area and are habitually late in finishing their evening meal, who are just so slow to eat, or whose disabilities meant they have to be fed?
- Would residents feel rushed out of Dining Room - in the way - before rehearsals?

"Could you email these points to me? I think one of the things that I could ask about at school would be the possibility of my friends doing a survey. If I presented it to the Business Administrator as a project about selecting music and added a few of the questions Brad was raising, then it might fly past her radar."

245

I studied my screen to decipher the proper keys to push and her phone pinged as she sat there.

"Got 'em," she said.

*

"Here are the results of our survey, Ma'am."

Margaret handed across a sheaf of paper with pie charts and graphs.

"You can see that the large majority of the residents enjoy the concerts both the organ ones and the augmented ones. You can see that they find the venue easy to access and would sooner attend a live performance than watch TV."

The Administrator scanned the results as Margaret took her through them nodding and agreeing that the addition of the students to the resident list and the concerts they brought had been worthwhile. The Administrator did not share the medical reports - they were anecdotal and private anyway but they backed up Margaret's survey.

"We sought input from the residents about the content of future concerts. We were surprised to see the mention of a Country and Western night, Fiddle contest, Pub nights, and request for outside choirs. There were numerous requests for attendance at additional cultural events like theatres and movies. We have a quartet of singers lined up to do Opera favourites but there were requests to visit the movie theatre for those live broadcasts."

"Well we have a residential bus that can take any who want to go to the movies," the Administrator replied as she scanned down the sheet until she hit the number. "Twenty-five!" she exploded. "The bus holds eight! This would sap all the staff we have to go to the theatre."

"We were surprised to see that as well. It seems you have a musical group here."

247

"Mr. Scottman is likely responsible for that. His musical concerts have been a favourite but I thought it was just filling in time.This looks like an infection has happened."

"I don't think that is a word I would have used to describe such enthusiastic interest."

Plainly caught off-guard, the Administrator frantically tried to backpedal, "I meant that in jest. I'm surprised to see such interest. We can't get a dozen to Bingo."

"There was a number of candid comments that we thought you should know about. They are at the bottom of the page."

Margaret directed the Administrator's attention beyond the chart. "You can see that there are many offered singly but there is a pattern. It seems that many seek any chance to get out of their rooms but not to attend many of the recreational options offered. The music has met a need among your residents, it seems."

"What reaction would there be to some of these other activities if they were actually to happen?"

the Administrator asked suspiciously.

"I would ask the residents. I'm sure they have thoughts."

"I'll bet they do," said the Administrator with tight lips. "Look at this list," she was focused back up the page. "A pub night? I wonder what liability insurance we'd have to have for that?"

"Well you could just send the bus out with any who wanted to attend the local watering hole, I suppose. I was there a bit ago when a men's choir came in after a performance at a nearby church. It was really fun. They sang for almost two hours - all sorts of pub songs. Can you imagine how that would go over here? Remember how the residents perked up over the baseball game when they were singing all those old songs? I'll bet most of the residents know most of those songs from their youth."

"I'll bet they'd all fall asleep - way past their bedtime, you know. They are all in pyjamas by nine usually."

"You might be surprised."

The administrator's eyes came up on that sentence, "Were some of our residents at that event?" she asked with narrowing eyes.

"I don't know everyone, but there were a lot of seniors besides the singers. Choristers are good models for people who could benefit from breathing exercises, or just because most of them so enjoy themselves when they sing. Fun can be … contagious, you know."

And Margaret didn't stop there.

"On the other hand, if you had a pub night in the residence, you'd have control over what everyone had to drink. I mean you know them all, right? You could serve them whatever would be OK for them. If they went to the Pub, they might sneak anything they wanted."

As she could see that sinking in, she added, "And anyone else would pay for drinks, right? I doubt you'd clear a thousand dollars on a night like that. Hardly worth the trouble."

*

"Did you really say that? The way you ended that presentation was downright devious. You're becoming a Senior before your time."

Brad was complimenting Margaret when the Brain-storming group met for a debriefing following the opera quartet concert. They were still at their tables that had been set up in cabaret style in the Dining Room.

The concert had ended with the drinking song from **La Traviata** and everyone had been able to swing a glass and toast at the end. Cheering took the place of clapping.

The principals took their bows and then stepped among the tables to mingle and accept the accolades that showered upon them. The Men's choir who had done the chorus part in the *Brindisi* as well as the *Anvil Chorus*, *Nun's Chorus*, and two from *Carmen*, headed directly down the side aisles for the bar set up at the back.

With a mug in hand, they mingled. It was no time before the drinking song from *Student Prince* started up a cappella, led by the tenor soloist in the choir pretending to woo the Business Administrator. She was blushing furiously as she became the focus of attention but rallied to accept the compliment graciously.

Thereafter, the spontaneous songs were similar to the ones the group had participated in at the Pub.

One Choir member stood to recite *Albert and the Lion*
and that set off another offering by Les Barker called *I'm
a lonely little lemming*. Margaret drew to the
Administrator's attention the absence of a single nodding
head in the audience and not a single early departure.
The lineup at the Administrator's door never stopped
next day asking when the next one was. The party
poopers secretly confessed to regretting that they missed
the evening.

Visitors over the next week found their way to the
Administrator's door as well, to comment on how alert
and excited their parents in the facility were about the
concert and had they heard correctly that the male voice
choir would be practicing weekly in the building and
allowing a silent audience to attend?

Three connected to the hospitality industry offered to
sponsor beverages after the rehearsals if their loved ones
could attend.

253

When the University Department of Studies in Aging called to ask if they could do a study of residents to connect emotional states like depression, loneliness, and forgetfulness to regular access to pub nights, it tipped the balance. It was becoming far too public and far too successful to decline.

Residents seemed to compete for a place in the various studies and traded bargaining rights like kids exchange hockey cards.

"I think that went well," Brad said to Margaret as the plan reached fruition. "We'd never have pulled that off with a committee. I wonder if the Administrator will ever figure out what we organized?" Brad asked.

"Well I won't tell," said Margaret.

"Me neither," Brad said. "What about you, Gerald?" he asked me. I mimed the monkey who spoke no evil.

21
THE CHARIOT

The flaw in our plan was the Administration's response to the return of Stuff. It was a ricochet shot. The aging study found that the institutional quality of the building had a debilitating effect on the residents. For many good reasons, halls and doorways had to be a certain width but they found positive benefits to resident outlook when rooms were customized to patients interests. Mine was held up as a model. And with that, stuff began to creep into the rooms.

"See? I told you," the Administrator was heard to be saying into the telephone. Well you could hardly miss the comment; her door was open, and she did say it loudly. Even those with hearing aids noticed.

The Administrator had a wheelchair - the residents called it *The Chariot*. It was old and huge and became the adjudicator of the battle in the war with administration over room furnishings. The Chariot had to be able to approach each side of the bed, or get into a closet, or bathroom. If it could do it, so could a stretcher or anything else they could imagine.

We had to apply to bring in any new furniture and the application required a cardboard cutout of the floor footprint of the piece. When it was laid on the floor, Administration would bring in the test machine to be driven through the spaces left. The test day was always announced with tones appropriate to Divine Judgment. The valiant fight put up by the Administrator was a worthy effort, most agreed but the woman had no idea who she was dealing with.

The Chariot had been left at the UnderCare Residence by someone who had 'gone on' in an earlier age. But that time was not out of the memory of some of us who had been there in the age of its creation. One of our number identified the make and model of The Chariot. He had sold them in his youth. He contacted friends still in the business and they resurrected one from a repair depot to which it had been relegated when parts were no longer available and from which it had not been junked. When the issue was explained, the staff at his old store flagged the relic, made it a museum piece for a display in the store, and brought it over, surreptitiously, whenever we needed it to test out a space before administration arrived.

If the treasure's footprint was found to occupy too much space and there was no other better place to situate it, we fixed the footprint by shaving off the cardboard till the wheelchair made it.

There was a limit to how much you could cut off. Another of our members had had a lengthy career in perceptual psychology and set the limits we could shave off and not get busted.

Doctor Emma Huggenburger never used her title. She found people expected her to have a stethoscope, but we all knew her background was in research. She was consulted on the visual aspects to make anything look smaller than it really was. The result was that the residents were never surprised. The Chariot always fit through the spaces required.

The desire for friendly things set off an active effort at deception. We seniors had an advantage because many of those who look after us really think we're all pretty addled. Yes, some have slipped past the point of no return, but many had not. Those capable of guile were not interested in changing people's perception of them.

They took to fudging the scores of the tests conducted to see if the new arrangements were improving us in various ways.

Emma knew many of the nuances of the tests that the young people brought to evaluate cognitive ability and mental processing speed. She held classes, on the sly, to prepare residents for how not to look too sharp and how to make the most of the weight of their comments about their emotional needs.

"They expect you to try your hardest and then that becomes the baseline for measuring the improvement," Dr. Emma coached. "If you look like you tried your best, but secretly didn't, can you see it's easier to get a higher score next time and make the change they are testing look better?" she asked.

Well, we figured that out in one, didn't we? We're not that stupid!

So, we consciously manipulated the scores we needed to make the changes look really good and we got the stuff that were the emblems of our lives back within our sight. And that felt really good. Almost every person found that they could sleep as well in a single bed if the space released meant they could rescue a favourite chair from the relative who had taken it, or a display cabinet of trinkets. Pictures returned to walls; neighbours visited each other's rooms as they had their homes, to admire favourite pictures back on the wall or symbols of significance displayed with pride.

And the missing and broken returned.

"Thank-you," said Eva when I met her in the hall with my bag of laundry. "I knocked a picture off the wall the other day when I went to get your neighbour's bedding. Glass all over the place. I can see another rule coming-no pictures with glass in them. Your idea of creating a poster that won't break is better."

I nodded and waved my departure to practice for the concert after lunch. But more stuff stories came up later.

"We've had a terrible time with another of the residents," Eva said as she gave me my meds and tucked me in.

She couldn't name the lady, but I knew who she was talking about.

261

"She's been collecting teacups from her neighbour. She used to run a fine china store and is convinced that her neighbour did not pay for the cups in her cabinet. They want to put her on medication because the old clerk is getting so upset."

I held up a hand, jumped out of bed and hustled into my change room. In my inner suitcoat pocket was the envelope of found money that beset me every week. I slapped it into Eva's hand and searched around for my iPad. I pecked out, *Found money. Antique store. Buy fifty C&S @ $2 ea. + old cabinet. Set up store in her room, Print receipts for neighbour? Mark cups?* I handed my marker pen to her with raised eyebrows.

"I don't know," said Eva, "I can suggest that. How much money is here?"

Enough, I tapped. *Do it on a day off, say a relative brought the stuff in.*

"I could get in trouble for this. But it would cost less than the meds and admin, and maybe do good things for the confused lady. I mean the money is a donation. Right?"

For that purpose only.

"I'll say that. But someone is going to say she requires too much time to look after such a thing."

Other patient? I pecked, *Administrator?*

Eva chuckled and having run out of objections, agreed.

"I like the last idea."

Later in the week a handsome cabinet with glass doors and sides mounted on long, curved, carved legs stood in pride of place beside the window in the Mrs. Pekot's room. It had been fitted with extra shelving between the wooden shelves to hold the cups and saucers. It was filled with the elegance of a by-gone day and Mrs. Pekot was telling us all that she had a new shipment for our inspection.

*

As the contest over stuff continued through the winter, I found myself of two minds. My kids had started the process of miniaturization that really replaced the concept of down-sizing.

 I didn't really miss the dining table you could play ping pong on, or the comfortable chairs that went with it, anymore. I felt at ease that all that had gone to someone who could use those things in their lives; the stuff was reborn and making around another turn with other people. That made me feel I had done the right thing, been a responsible steward of a part of the world's wealth that had fallen to me. What I had not wanted to give up had, in fact, stayed with me but in a digital form. My whole past was collected on something the size of my thumb. I still felt humbled by that.

I could access my music faster than I had ever been able to. That was astounding. If I forgot my glasses when I got to the organ, I could move the cursor to three hundred percent instead - another amazement. But I still have a collection of pencils to the right of the keyboard beside my earphones, and a pack of post-it notes to jot down details I fear I will forget. Some habits die hard, I guess.

Many of my fellow residents seemed restored once they were allowed to bring the tangibles of their past into and onto their walls. Yes, the clutter created a cleaning problem, but the deal had been that anything not institutional had to be cleaned or dusted under supervision during a bed-making or it had to be surrendered. That was motivation enough.

And the staff commented on how it seemed to keep memories fresh as the residents did it. What a surprise! Obviously, the staff did not grow up with the tangibles of generations past whose accomplishments and

memorabilia were reviewed and cleaned, every Saturday
of their young lives.

Our monitors and measurers documented that the items
that residents chose to share with others often stimulated
positive and energetic responses from others and the
results were meaningful conversations that blossomed
into friendships.

But between breakages, misplacements, and sometimes
thefts, the Administration found the return of stuff to be a
series of problems no matter how well it made their
clients feel. The residents felt the imbalance of influence,
some more than others. If all you have are memories, and
the tools to restore them, you seem to be no match for
organized institutional minimalism and single solutions.
The contest honed in my fellow residents, a political
savvy and passive resistance that I would never have
imagined.

When the men's choir began to use the Dining Room as a
rehearsal hall and the Sitting Room, thereafter, for drinks

with the residents its membership increased and soon the adult children and the grandchildren of our residents were suddenly among those on stage.

I was particularly impressed by a group of women who sequentially arranged for the corporate bus to take them to their children's houses just before bedtime.

They were most creative in the reasons that such late transport was required.

"Shift work keeps my daughter at the hospital till late," one said. "It's the only time I can get into the house to get my next season's wardrobe or talk about my investments or … whatever."

Another had to visit grandchildren who were promised a visit with grandma only after schoolwork was done.

"I wouldn't want to disappoint them," said the septuagenarian.

I bought something today at the mall, and I must return it before they close at ten, almost didn't work but she had done her homework and the store did close late. The whole point of these ruses was to be sure any choristers who might have had a drop too much and didn't pass the breathalyzer that the ladies had in a purse, had a ride home. As long as the driver was taking them, could they drop off … And of course, the women got to gossip later about the guys they had to drive home.

The scuttlebutt I caught amongst the choir members focussed on a different aspect of those moments.

"If you have that second beer, the Black Mariahs will be taking you home. Want to explain that to your wife?" The whole dynamic had the desired effect on consumption.

Community social media visits needed a separate calendar. A committee formed to greet, direct and be interviewed. Of course, the team had press releases in hand. The news spread further when a women's choir filled another night for their group to practice. A steady stream of selfies sent by residents attracted the regular media. More interviews happened; documentary cameras seemed to be requesting access in a never-ending line. It was a new use that we residents discovered for the encyclopedic experience that we possessed among ourselves compared to the myopic and narrow experience of the residence owners.

Politicians were regularly invited to share concert events and use the seniors for a photo op. The underground organizing committee made sure the Administration looked so progressive and aware of the needs of seniors in their programming. *Leaders in the Field* they were called in the handouts that seniors slipped to reporters while transferring their own contact information and suggesting they were inside sources.

22

THE MEMORY

"You know I used to admire the certainty all that information you have in that computer, gives you. In the time some take to phrase a sentence, you have facts that would peel paint off a wall, they're so boring. And they are so authoritative, absolutely irrefutable."

Brad waved at the widescreen monitor on the music stand of my organ, "With that, you connect to people you never knew across time and space. Day after day, you flawlessly recreate magical moments from some of the greatest minds who ever lived from the stuff they left. You write down everything important in your life in that ledger."

It stood open on the top of the organ waiting for me to record what I'd done and how well.

"If I asked you when you last played Bach's A minor concerto, you could tell me with a flick of your finger on that keyboard. You could turn to the page in this tome," his hand thumped on it as he spoke, "and you would tell me all the mistakes you made as you played and where the organ was. Do you know you are the only person in this place who comes from such a certain past?"

I stopped playing. He had shocked me with his statement, as though I had done something wrong. We were putting in time till we were called for our dental appointments. Our summons came over the Public address system.

"Everyone here," he said as we walked, "can pick up a picture and tell you who the people are, where it was taken, what they ate on the picnic. But you know what? There isn't another soul who can verify what they claim. I think that is another virtue of the stuff we've collected and the meanings we attach to it."

We looked out on the frozen garden as we passed down the hallway.

"You can tell me more than I ever wish to know about any concert you've played in, the name of organists the world over, not because you remember them, but because you wrote it down. If I asked what you had for breakfast that day, with complete certainty, you could tell me because you always have the same breakfast. But is it possible that they ran out of porridge that day? Would you remember if it happened?" His comments left me wondering how I did recall any other memorable moments. But he wasn't finished.

"For all the rest of us, I think I could make a case for us making up either intentionally or accidentally, many of the memories we claim are connected to the stuff we so admire and which might have burdened our lives thus far. I can give an example. You know my ebony statue - Jonas?"

How could anyone forget the only piece except clothing, he took from his apartment. I nodded.

"Well I was convinced that Jonas and I bought it from Isaac Edokpolo. I could tell you the day, and the workshop - draw you a picture of the place if you'd asked. I can see Jonas posing for the drawing Isaac made for the carving - the slant of the sun through the window. It was one of the absolute certainties in my life - until the statue got knocked over during cleaning yesterday. On the bottom it is signed by the carver and that man's name is Vincent Ihaza! So how could I have made such a mistake for so long?"

"Did his student, Vincent, do the actual carving?"

"Vincent had his own studio on the other side of town," he replied in exasperation.

273

"So it makes me think that others may have the same issue. The stuff we have keeps our minds active as we do the associations every time we look at them. That has to be helpful to seniors like me, but somewhere, somewhen, I cross-connected two memories to create a wrong recollection. Now nobody knows or cares but me. It has just unhinged me. Is this the first step in the slide into forgetfulness?

I rummaged through my pockets and found a spare pad of Post-its and a blunt pencil and pushed it over.

He scowled at them and declined, "I think I'd rather make it up," he replied as he slid them back.

"Having now decided on a future unfettered by fact, what's else is on the agenda today? They said that these were the golden years, but I had no idea how liberating they could be."

I held the door to the medical suite where the dental team looked all too happy to see us.

"How you doing?" the assistant asked.

Brad and I looked at each other and shook our heads.

"I presume that is a rhetorical question," Brad replied.

The assistant looked puzzled. Brad headed towards the dental chair. I took a seat in the waiting area.

23
MRS. BERESFORD

Maybe that is why I've never composed anything of my own; all I do is recreate what geniuses before me, have. I am fixated on documentation. I want to be absolutely sure and in those musical notations there is what I seek. Well I'm no such genius but I think I see what they were trying to say and feel content in just deciphering for those who never knew these musicians of the past as well as I do, the message in the medium.

Brad was looking smug and drawing breath as though his argument was the last word before he went to have his teeth checked. My appointment had been shorter. He was now ready to resume our discussion with almost an hour of deliberation to back it up.

He had declared my life rigidly regulated by the medium I was consumed by. He was not the only one who had had time to think; before he could speak, I held up a restraining hand. It had scribbled out, on my recovered Post-it pad, *Rhapsody on a THEME from Paganini.* Below it I wrote, *Brother can you spare a dime, variations, Choir variations on variations, Twinkle, Twinkle.*

"So, you're saying that those scores are not as absolute as I think? Aren't they treated as holy writ? Who changes a chord in a piece, and it isn't called a mistake?"

Need to give credit, I wrote.

"OK, I get that; if someone wrote a piece, he or she deserves to have it followed if their name is on it."

I could see we had to go back to the organ if I was going to make my point.

I powered it up and gave him his earphones. I took middle C and played the C Major scale. I counted off for him the number of notes, white and black, in the space of the C scale - thirteen. Then it was back to my notepad.

Next note? I wrote when I played middle C.

"D," he said.

Need to know. Is C starting note or next to last? Or two from end? I wrote.

I gave him the rules by which notes make major scales - Tone, Tone, Semitone, Tone, Tone, Tone, Semitone, and picked out the keys as I did.

Suppose C is next to last note of scale, the one after it would be...? I scribbled.

He was about to say when I pointed to the rule.

"If C was the next to last note of a major scale, the last note would be a semitone up - that would be C#," he figured slowly.

If C is second to last, ... last note is? I wrote.

He pushed me aside to follow the pattern tentatively to D#.

"So, there are a lot of choices for where to go in making up a melody?"

I struggled how to tell him that D# was also called E♭. I nodded then wrote, *Did I mention minor keys as well?*

"You're giving me the abridged version?"

I nodded and held up fingers pinched to a tiny space between.

Next note determined by key signature one starts with. I wanted to tell him that each starting note has a key signature that tells players what the next note will be. Instead I played a raft of scales in different key signatures, all of which included the note called middle C.

"So how do you decide which key signature to play in?"

I held a hand over my heart.

"Are you saying that emotion governs the key you write a song in?"

I nodded and started to play *Twinkle, Twinkle* in a minor key.

"That is sad," he said.

I stopped and waved my hand to keep going.

"There are other criteria?"

I nodded again, and played **Twinkle** majestically, then like a music box.

Brad seemed to consider a moment, "You're telling me that there are a lot of combos for putting notes together?"

I nodded and wrote, *Millions, Billions.*

I was down to my last few Post-its, *Melody is a path through Regulation Land - makes you feel something. Can't lose the map if you want to repeat it. Close doesn't count. But can always make up new based on earlier theme using the rules.*

I shook my hand it was so cramped from my writing then I played *Can you spare a dime* variations. I stopped, shook my hands again and pointed towards the tables.

Dinner smells were coming from the door to the kitchen.

But over dinner, Brad's thoughts hit home.

"Maybe it was time to become a little more creative. Yes, a lot of my life was spent following well-worn tracks in a musical landscape pointing out the attractions to any who would share the trip. Was it time to blaze another path of my own? Maybe I could create a ... how did Brad say it? ... a less fettered future. The music I was working with all day, every day, offered the chance. Maybe such creations could replace the stuff I'd given up or the way to feel better about having given it up."

*

"She had so much stuff and it was gorgeous. The choir I belonged to was invited to her place when I was a kid. I remember my mouth fell open. I mean the shine on the antique chairs and tables was an inch deep," said Jessica as she spoke to her roommate in the lounge.

They were coated, hatted, and booted for the weather and were waiting for a taxi to get them to a private gig they had arranged at another opulent home - background duets for dinner, I'd heard.

I joined the conversation late and drew a question mark in the air to ask who they were talking about.

"Mrs. Beresford," Jessica continued. "I thought I recognized her in the audience at the concert and after, I went to be sure. I told her how much we enjoyed visiting her home back fifteen, maybe twenty years ago."

"She was pleased to talk to me then, but I gather from the staff that she is one unhappy camper these days."

I drew another question mark.

"Well, she used to be the envy of everyone for all the things she had, and it was all so beautiful."

A sigh escaped with the memory, "If you got it, you flaunt it right? Well she did and loved the adulation that went with it. In her world, stuff counted. It occupied your space. The radiation killed anything close; it said, *'look how valuable I am because I can have all these things.'* So, for whatever reason, she doesn't have all those things now. The crowds have stopped talking about her. Even in the short time I spoke with her the other night, you could see she lit up when I mentioned that house. I left after I heard the third regret that all her things were gone now, and she was just dumped here to die. If you don't have stuff, you don't count, in her life, it seems. Oh., our ride is here," she added.

They scooped up their instruments and jumped up. I waved goodbye with a thumbs up salute.

They laughed and waved back.

The conversation brought a whole litany of past feelings bubbling back up.

The loss of all my life keepsakes still squeezed me. I can go to my room with all the musicians of my past staring down on me as I fall asleep. I can meet my family, back for three generations, in my dressing room closet. But those are the only places where my space says I belong - this is mine.

It is all an illusion. It only takes Eva to arrive with her cart to remind me that I'm really living in someone else's space. Whether it is the cart in the doorway or her scent in the air, it is all the reminder I need to recall that this is not mine, and I'll die here. I guess as long as you have your own stuff, you can more effectively deny the passage of time. Maybe that is Mrs. Beresford's real problem; it's not really the loss of the bulwark of stuff that was fortifying her against what is happening to everyone else, it is being unable to accept that she isn't different. She has no defense now. So, she cycles between the remnants of her life, as I once did. It makes for a depressing existence.

I learned a while ago that I feel a lot better if I confront such confinement by doing something and that, of course, takes me into my music. It is escaping in all the senses of that word. But from that space I can return with something that others enjoy. It is what drives me to continue to prepare the notes for Sunday services, my mini concerts, the choir. I'm beginning to sound somewhat obsessive. *I wonder if m'lady has music in her past? I'll have to ask about her.*

I decided to return to my room and there, in isolated splendour on the synths-piano, was my iPad. *"The kids look up all kinds of details on those things, I wonder if I can?"* I thought.

I turned it on and found the search icon. I looked at the blinking cursor for a while wondering what to do next but presumed the keyboard was there for a reason, so I pecked in Mrs. Beresford and waited.

"Holy Smoke! Is she Mrs. Lillian Beresford?" If she is her parents rebuilt and expanded the pipe organ at a church where I had served, decades back. And then financed the addition to the building as well. Everyone thought they had more money than God.

24
THE CONFESSION

I guess I'd forgotten to pull the partition back to screen me from the room. Maybe nobody had told her about the etiquette of not bothering me when I was practicing. Maybe Mrs. Beresford didn't expect to be excluded from anywhere she wanted to go. Didn't matter, I just know that when she reached up to change the page on the paper score on the music stand, I jumped.

I'd been concentrating so hard on the fingering and footwork I needed to master to play the Schubert piece that the girls wanted to do as a trio that when she reached up to turn the page … I had to draw a breath to calm down - several in fact.

"Did I startle you?" she asked. Surely it was a rhetorical question.

I smiled when I caught me breath and reached out a handout to shake hers. She returned a limp response with surprise. *"Do people not shake your hand?"* I wondered. I looked past her to see I had closed the screens to the room. *"What's she doing here?"* I wondered.

"I feel lost in this place," she announced, waving a hand beyond the screens. "I've seen you on a couple occasions come in or leave this space. I wondered what you were doing. Are you really practicing?"

I nodded.

"And you can't speak. But you can hear, right?"

I nodded.

"Well maybe you can be a confessor for me. If you can't speak, any secret would be safe right?"

I reached across and picked up my stubby pencil at the end of the keyboard.

As I was raising it between us, she snatched it from my fingers and in a blink stuffed it down the front of her dress.

I was shocked! I wasn't sure if I was supposed to go after it, or if it was the only way she could convey her desperate need to share something troubling. I guess my mouth fell open before I regained my poise.

I acknowledged her win and held up my hands in surrender. I don't know what I expected but she caught me off-guard again by asking if she could use the other pair of earphones coiled at the end of the keyboard and listen while I practiced some more.

I was a bit reluctant to reveal my failings but there was something in her manner that cried out. I paused for a moment then passed them over. She hooked a hip over the end of the bench. I went back to the part which was giving me grief. I don't know how long it took me but I finally got it right enough to know my fingers and feet would do what they had to without my thinking about them.

I backed up and ran through the troublesome part, then went even further back and took a longer run. That required the page turn and she did it for me, right on time, without my nod. We did it a couple more times and I was about to stop when she turned further on in the score and stopped at one of the most thrilling phrases in the piece.

"Would you play this passage?" she asked.

I set my hands in place and closed my eyes.

In my head I could hear the notes of the page before and when my mind let me, I entered firmly and then progressed upward dragging on the time just enough to make it painfully beautiful - as soul-twisting as the composer had intended. I was about to continue on when she put a hand on mine.

"I can go back to my room, happy now. That was truly beautiful."

She stood and gave me back her earphones.

As I put my own back and locked up the instrument, I realized that she hadn't winced once at my discords. She didn't complain a whit when my foot clipped her ankle. I gestured towards the tables where we could wait for the tea wagon.

She led the way to the furthest corner of the room, where we sat with our backs to the room.

"I've never been so lonely in my life," she began. "I've been dumped here, incarcerated by a family that has stripped my of every financial support I ever had. I'd call it elder abuse brought on by having the better things in life that others covet. You'd never prove it with the legal help they have but it's true nonetheless." She smouldered a moment while I tried to decide if these are the ravings of deranged matriarch. "But I have a few tricks yet," she muttered.

She jerked back to the room we were in, "They tell me everyone feels like this at the start. You have to get to know people. Well there are few people I've met here that I really want to know. Their lives and mine have not intersected for a lifetime. I wouldn't know what to say to them. I hope you might be a person I could talk to because you can't talk back or tell others easily. I hope you realize how valuable a quality that is to me." She looked steadily at me.

I looked down and nodded.

"Sounds like I've been damned but with faint praise," I thought.

"And the other quality you possess is that you let me share your struggle a moment ago." She flipped her head back towards the organ. "You could have told me to go to hell and thrown a tizzy-fit. I had just barged into your sanctum, uninvited. I don't mean the floor space behind the partitions. I barged into your mind space and you let me stay. So that tells me you are not afraid for others to see you mess up because you are confident in your ability to finally succeed. I would so love to have that ability, that confidence."

I put a hand on hers as they twisted on the table.

"I used to play but I could not bear the thought that anyone would see me make a mistake, so I stopped. My parents wanted too badly for me to succeed. It was what genteel women did - learned to play a musical instrument."

She continued, "It was a carryover from their own childhood, maybe their grandparents. Who knows? They wanted me to learn the piano, but I was paralyzed by my fear. To hide that, I said I wanted to take up the Violin. I was in my teens then and they bought me the best money could buy. Within a year, I announced with all the arrogance a debutante could muster, that I would rather learn the cello. Again, the best in the world arrived and I was trapped into more lessons that proved again, my failure to accept failure. I got married and have not touched those instruments since, but they are still in my room. I insisted they come with me. They are in a leather-bound steamer trunks. I wanted them to remind me of a moment when I could tell the world I would not do their bidding. They are symbols of my resistance," Her voice was quivering and down to a whisper.

She sighed, "But they have become a monument to arrogance that embarrasses me. I am so alone because of everything they represent about my life. They are gorgeous instruments."

She caught her breath and wiped away a tear, "They were given to me to inspire me and then to beat me with. Instead of acknowledging my inability, I scorned what others would have died for. I flipped my finger at them all. It was so satisfying to sneer." Her words vibrated with a flash of arrogance before fading.

"I am not worthy to touch them, because I wouldn't try like you do. I haven't the courage or belief in myself and they stand there, those two cases, mocking me every moment."

I had been swept into the emotion of a tortured soul who called from absolute isolation. I patted her hand to try to calm her twisting. I was trying to process what she was saying and how sorry I was for her musical training that had left her so bitter and now so remorseful. I found myself replaying her words and…*"What had she said ?"*

I guess my head must have cocked as I processed the meaning in her confession. I lifted my head slowly to look into those anguished eyes and I'm afraid my eyes were opening to match my mouth.

"Yes," she acknowledged. "A cello and a violin. The best that money can buy. And I'm ashamed to say I own them."

I was still wide-eyed at what she was really saying. *Was she saying what I thought?*

She nodded again, confirming my guess, and barely whispered, "Yes."

I've lost track of time when I was engrossed in my music sometimes. This was the first time it had happened when my hands were not on a keyboard. I realized I'd been holding my breath too long and took a lungful.

I had to find my notepad. I patted her hand to remain seated and went back to the organ for Post-its and another pencil.

When I came back, I wrote, *who's looking after them?*

"Nobody, for more than fifty years," she answered and hung her head.

Now what? I wrote.

"I was hoping you would know. Just being able to share this has been a huge relief," but she started to twist her hands again.

Discretion needed, I wrote.

"Of course," she replied somewhat imperiously.

I'll enquire? I wrote.

"Please do," she replied but it wasn't a directive, it was an appeal.

I pointed to the tea caddy that had clattered into the room behind us.

"Oh, they only serve the most terrible tea and the biscuits are appalling."

I mimed that I would return with better cookies.

"While you do that, I'll see if I can teach the staff how to make tea properly. I have my own blend in my room. Can we meet back here?"

I nodded. Before I returned with Margaret 's gingerbread cookies, I texted Jessica. *Urgent need to talk. Bring your luthier. Bring Head of Music Dept.*

*

Jessica and Margaret had joined me for supper and could hardly eat for their excitement. Jessica was gushing,

"Here, hold this," she said, "and gave me her Stradivarius Violin! I mean when in my life will that happen again? They were looking for a business card that might have been inside the case to see who looked after it for her back then. The violin maker and Department Head were all a twitter when they found it and I just stood there with that multi-million-dollar violin in my hands! I could see the marking inside through the 'f' hole. I mean that was put in there over three hundred years ago! What do you have to do to be able to play something like that?"

"Practice, practice, practice?" suggested Margaret.

She had tagged along when the group moved off to Mrs. Beresford's room to be sure that what the old lady was talking about was not the figment of a senior's imagination.

Margaret had been last into the small room and so caught in the passage to the bed area where the violin was laying. She found herself looking into the dressing area where the cello stood in a stand. While everyone else had clustered around the bed, she sidestepped into the space, past the antique dresser covered with a lace doily and crowded against the dressing table, to touch the instrument. It was a little lighter in colour than hers. There were a few scratches in the finish. A shaggy bow hung in the rest on the back of the stand, many of the hairs were broken and hanging down.

"*Where have you been,*" she thought. *What could you tell me?*"

While the buzz of conversation continued in the adjacent room, Margaret felt like she was looking at a body in a casket at a visitation.

In real life, she and a cello had a common language but neither this instrument nor she was able to reach across what separated them now. Even touching it brought no response. It was just cool and smooth.

Margaret stepped back into the entry before Mrs. Beresford declared, "The cello is in here."

The whole crowd around the bed, reversed field. Mrs. Beresford passed through them like a ship at full power, her bow wave lifting aside all in her path.

"You can't all come in here," she directed. Let me bring it out." Margaret backed further out of the room into the hall so Mrs. Beresford and her priceless cello could move back to the bed area, where Jessica must have just put the violin down. The cello joined it on the bedspread.

Margaret realized she'd been not paying attention and quickly asked, "I guess they can't tell much about the bow until it is re-haired. How did you find out she had two Stradivarius instruments, Mr. Scottman?"

I just smiled and held my fingers to my lips and made a Shhh sound.

"What will happen to them now?" Jessica asked.

"I heard the Head of the Music Department suggesting they be transferred into a foundation. Mrs. Beresford would be a trustee, perhaps the only one, or she could name co-trustees to help decide on how to use these things. There is no doubt that they'll require some technical attention, immediately, before they go out on the road so to speak. So, the foundation needs some financial capital to cover that and probably storage, insurance policies, that sort of stuff."

I pulled out my Post-it pad and wrote, *Want to be a trustee?* and showed it to both of them.

"What do you have to do?" asked Jessica.

I shrugged.

Margaret replied, "Well you have to make decisions about who gets the instruments, for how long, why, that sort of thing. I would guess you become the object of lobbying efforts from different factions who would convince you of the virtues of their cause. I would expect you have to figure out how to work with people you never worked with and whose decision-making process you have never needed to know…Not much."

Jessica flashed a look at the ceiling. "Right," she said sarcastically. Then in a curious tone she asked, "Does it pay?"

Both looked at me. I shrugged.

"It might mean you become known as the lady who decides futures, who is the gate-keeper to lifetime chances, the lady who sank someone's career," suggested Margaret.

"Not sure I like the sound of that. On what criteria could anyone decide things like that?" asked Jessica. "If you became a trustee," she looked squarely at Margaret, "figuring out such stuff would be top of your list. But you've got library research skills up the yahoo. I'll bet you could find out how other foundations do things like this. It isn't as though there aren't a bunch of instruments by this builder still around and being played. How did those people get to do that?"

I looked at Margaret's face as Jessica was talking. I could see the wheels working already.

25
WHAT DO YOU DO WITH IT

"I accepted conditionally to be a trustee on Mrs. Beresford's committee," Margaret admitted as she sat with Brad and I at dinner. "If I don't like the job, or it gets in the way of my other priorities, I can resign. So, I have a two-year contract."

"It'll take almost that time to get the instruments back into playing condition, I'd guess," Brad said as he polished his plate with the last bite of his bun.

"The luthier says maybe half that. Anyone who gets it will need time to get used to it as well so first public concerts will be about the time I have to decide if I'll stay on or change.

I held up my finger to my lips.

"You think I should keep my membership a secret?" Margaret asked.

I nodded.

"I thought it would be something to put on my CV."

Brad interrupted, "I think he's saying that those who don't get to play the instruments, might carry a grudge that could cost you in other ways - like personal career progress etc."

I nodded.

"Very accomplished musicians can sometimes have a diva complex, you know. They really want everything their way. Mrs. Beresford was likely a good example in her day. So, I think what Gerald is saying is that you might just keep your membership under your hat for a while. Once you let it out, you can't call it back.

Remember the warning of the whaler; they can only harpoon you while you're spouting."

"Where do you get those sayings?" Margaret asked Brad.

"There is a book of them at the Public ..."

I jabbed him sharply in the ribs. He shouldn't lead the gullible along like that.

"...Library," he continued, sliding out of my reach.

"We're talking about how to decide who gets to play them. Mrs. Beresford drags out the discussion into a week of casual meetings in the hall or after dinner. If anyone gets an idea, they write it in a notebook in her room."

Margaret gathered her thoughts before she proceeded.

"I came in with how other foundations decide. They come to a decision mostly through a competition that promotes the foundation and makes a big splash in the community. The question then becomes who plays best. You're asking a group of seniors with questionable hearing, to judge intonation? The idea really makes me wonder. Anyway, I was all ready to share the products of my research. I had it all printed out and Mrs. Beresford just tucked it into the notebook and asked if there was anything else. I felt dismissed."

She cut off Brad's attempt at interruption by barging on.

"Sometimes they put the players behind a screen to attempt to focus on the auditory qualities of their audition instead of the visual. Some of these people are very attractive, you know."

I didn't know that but couldn't comment anyway.

"Anyway, after thinking about it, I wonder if such a violin or cello would ever get into young hands if they had to compete. I don't know if a young player needs something like that to scratch out a tune. Seems like tossing a pearl into a pig pen."

I shook my head to try to say I disagreed.

"Anyway, when the information approaches some critical mass, I guess a meeting will be called to decide what to do. In the meantime, Jessica gets to play scales on it each day. *She's the trainer*, she says, *who has to get the instrument back into condition now it's been repaired.* The cello will take a while before its back from the luthier."

"Who else is on the Board of Trustees?"

"There is a lawyer and a banker who seem to be friends of Mrs. Beresford," she continued.

"She asked the Music Department Head and I hear she wants to invite the Concert Master of the Orchestra. She also said she was looking for someone who performs in the Country and Western music scene and who plays the fiddle."

"The last one looks like the lady is thinking outside the box," Brad observed.

"It gives me hope I'll not be the token young person and beyond that that there might be a place for a weird idea I had about how to find someone to play the thing."

Jessica came in and was hailed to join us. Everyone shuffled over to make space and while that happened, we cleared our dishes and brought back coffees.

"Margaret was about to share a weird idea," Brad said when we'd all settled.

We all looked at her.

"OK, but don't say I didn't warn you." She looked around at smiling faces. "I wonder if playing the violin might be a small part of the decision-making process. It seems to be the only priority in these other foundations. But I wonder if there is anything besides playing that counts."

Everyone looked expectantly as she waited in silence. I waved her on.

"Suppose the player was just dirt poor, or played in pubs, or was someone just starting out."

"Like Mrs. Beresford?" asked Brad. "Someone gave her that instrument and all she did was store it, under her dress."

I touched Brad's hand to stop him.

No, I did not say under her dress. She hid it as a protest - 'duress' was the word, I wrote.

He looked happy that someone had recognized his attempt at humour.

"No. The instrument goes to someone who is obsessive and who plays all the time, or learns to," continued Margaret. "They may not be the world's best, but they play in front of ordinary people for the joy of it."

"Like the guy who saws away outside the door to the Mall? I've never seen him play a single melody. He just saws back and forth in rhythm with the recording coming out of the speaker," Brad said.

"No, I mean someone who is passionate, but will never make the big stage, someone who makes mistakes, who teaches kids in a string program after hours at school."

She paused for a moment.

"I once heard that a world-famous violinist played his Strad in a Subway arcade and two people in the thousand that passed in forty-five minutes noticed enough to appreciate what they were hearing. Is that because they never heard anything so good and didn't recognize it when they heard it?"

"So, you need someone who is obsessed with teaching people to listen," Brad summarized "Wonder where you'd find somebody like that?" He swung to stare pointedly at me.

I pulled out my Post-its. *Need two hands. Not playing with feet*, I scribbled.

"Whenever you give this man a challenge he just wimps out. Have you noticed that?" Brad retorted after reading out my note. He found everyone looking at him.

Brad blushed.

He realized he'd just trapped himself into explaining why he should not be such a teacher to the auditorily challenged.

"I will plead seniority that produces too small a return on investment. It needs a younger person."

At which point we all looked at Jessica.

"Well, you are working it into shape already," Margaret said. "Why not become Ms. Stradivarius. Have string thing - will travel."

Jessica blushed and pushed past the double entendre.

"Well, how do I pay my rent and food bill? If all you do is free concerts to people who can't tell one note from another, are you just suggesting I set out a hat?"

"As I recall the virtuoso found the same problem.

He got one big donation, but most people put in change. People value only what they pay for, it seems. It's about money. The status of an expensive car is that it costs a lot and others know that, not that it gets you to work any faster."

"So, you think public Strad concerts wouldn't raise the public appreciation of music?" Margaret concluded.

"Well it didn't when that guy did it in the Subway."

"I recall hearing of another virtuoso who took a violin from a beggar on the street one day and make it sound like a million bucks playing the exact tune the amateur had been playing. I wonder if the beggar ever played again after he'd been made to realize how badly he was playing."

"It was a couple years ago I heard of a busker who played classical stuff on the street for years and can't wait to do it again."

"Does he have a Strad?"

"I doubt."

"There is a body of people who do argue that even good musicians can't pick out a Strad from other good violins in blind tests. Well if they can't, why would we expect ordinary people to be able to. And doesn't this make the whole Strad thing a difference in the mind - a mystique?"

"OK so we've beaten this to death. Maybe there is only one place for a Strad and it's on a concert stage played by one of the world's best to some of the world's wealthiest. I think that's wimping out, but it is so defensible and so widely accepted, how could it be wrong?" Margaret was frustrated but seemed reluctantly resigned.

But it seemed to me she had not given up on a place for a Strad at a grass-roots level.

*

I was musing on Margaret 's conflict over what to do with a Stradivarius violin when the author of her problem suddenly bumped me over on the organ bench, some days later. I continued to doodle around swinging my feet across the pedal board making up harmonies as I went, simply demonstrating that Mrs. Beresford could not interrupt whenever she wanted. Without earphones, I made her wait till authority had been established.

"I thought you might be here," she said. The woman has a talent for stating the obvious.

I nodded as I took off my earphones.

"I'm beginning to regret asking that young lady to join the Trustees. Fortunately, it is only for two years."

The comment was designed to get my attention. I looked up at the ceiling, back at her, and rolled a wave to get her to continue. I had music to play.

"Do you know she had the gall to suggest that if we were serious about encouraging young musicians, we should SELL the violin once its value has been determined?"

The word fairly exploded out of her. A mist of spit sprayed into the air and settled slowly towards the top rank of keys on the organ.

I looked up doing some mental arithmetic, but I didn't need to. Mrs. Beresford was waving a much-wrinkled piece of paper.

"Look at this," she ordered.

I took it. As I scanned down the page of estimates, Mrs. Beresford kept up her monologue.

"If the violin were sold at what the current market would bear, tens of millions of dollars would change hands. She estimates with the proceeds of the sale, we could pay the tuition of about four hundred students at the university level every year forever using only the interest of the money from the sale. Are there even four hundred students of stringed instruments in the country at that level?"

Her voice was rising throughout her delivery; she snatched back the paper from me.

"And look at these conclusions. Still have capital to buy another Strad." She pointed with her finger at the next line, "And here. Still have the cello."

I waggled my head back and forth to try to suggest the plan had merit and was worth considering further. My mind was wandering back to some of the last chords I'd been playing when she interrupted.

I picked up my Post-it pad and scribbled, *sounds good.*

"Ohhhh," she exploded in outrage.

I plucked the paper from her hand. When she reached for it back, I stuffed earphones into her hand and tossed the page over my shoulder. I pointed to the score on the screen on my music stand. The end of the fugue that was displayed needed all hands and feet to play it. I pointed to her end of the keyboard and ran my hand and feet through the last line to that chord.

I knew she could play both hands of the last chord and she could sense I was about to pull my hand away to let her do it. She stiffened as her entry slowly approached. Her fingers were in place over the correct notes as I hit the penultimate ones and then just as I lifted my hand and hit the proper pedals, she intentionally shifted her hands slightly to play the minor key to end the piece.

It was not what I expected but it was an interesting end.

With a snap nod of her head toward the music she spat out, "There!" slid off the bench and stalked out of my practice space.

I figured that was about as elegant a statement as I'd get that this discussion had not ended. Things were still hanging just as the notes had said.

When I locked up, the proposal paper was still on the floor; I picked it up to return it to her later.

*

Jessica button-holed me as I sat in the Sitting Room listening to the Men's Choir rehearse in the Dining Area. I guess I was just staring at the garden outside the window where a row of daffodils was getting ready to bloom, each set of leaves standing beside a numbered wooden slat. Brad had started a lottery getting residents to buy tickets on when the first of all would bloom, which one would bloom first in each clump, date of the last bloom, I couldn't keep up with the number of categories he'd created. It cost a dollar a bet. I just gave him a twenty and told him to put me down for whatever of each. Winners would get credits to their bar bill. Money raised would go to the Alzheimer's Society, or the Cancer Society depending on the vote in progress among the residents.

When Jessica spoke, I'd been mentally playing *All in an April Evening*. The Choir had been singing it well, accompanied by their pianist. I just couldn't help mentally playing it as well.

"I was called in by the Research Team Leader, as a courtesy, when they talked with Management about the results of the ongoing study of the place as a result of the changes that have happened. You should have been there really; you started this. I just brought in the Psychs to see if the effort could pressure the Administration to expand the program. It's way out of my hands but they asked me just to be nice, I think."

I applauded gently on the table with one hand.

"You'd have been impressed with the anecdotes in their report," she continued.

I cocked my head to show my interest.

"I guess a couple of the Choir members have moved a senior relative in here as a result of coming to practice here and seeing the services and layout. I think they are about at capacity now. They might even be thinking an expansion."

I smiled.

"The word is getting around that this place is really a home rather than a warehouse.

I nodded.

"The Doctor mentioned that there have been improvements in many cognitive scores but how much seems in doubt. I think they are questioning the validity of the starting scores."

My mouth dropped open in surprise.

"They think there might have been a conscious effort to misrepresent abilities at the outset so that the changes looked more dramatic"

I sat back, feigning shock and put a hand over my heart.

"But there is no doubt that the pub night is a social success. Two of the ladies, no names please, were mentioned to have started to wear makeup and dress up for the drinks that the men have after practice."

Both our eyes turned to the un-named pair across the lounge who were waiting patiently for the last chords of *Ave Verum*. One checked her watch for the third time.

"The doctor thinks they have crushes on a couple of the choristers."

Chatter had replaced the singing across the hall. Practice had ended. Residents could now join the men for a drink if they wished and there was no doubt that many did. But the pair of women across the room was leading the rush.

Jess and I joined the movement into the Dining Area.

The bar had finally figured out that making people line up at the bar was a non-starter. They put pitchers on each table. Men served themselves in a fraction the time so there was more time for socializing. The different brews were labelled on different tables. To get a drink, they picked up their glasses at the bar and handed over their drink tickets then. They'd bought their tickets beforehand at their intermission or before practice.

When the maestro called to me, Jessica took my tickets to get us glasses. I handed her an extra one for the musician.

"We're finally getting sixteenth notes," the conductor said as we raised our mugs in a toast, "but I swear that teaching them syncopation or semitones is like teaching birth control to rabbits."

I nodded and smiled in agreement. Jessica then fell to chatting with him about her playing her violin in place of the soprano solo in *Nun's Chorus* in an upcoming concert.

I just watched the various combinations around the room. Because everyone could get a glass and beverage that recognized their medicines and conditions, it was a happy time for all. How could it be otherwise? It was the night nurse doing bar keeping. She knew who the diabetics were. She had carbonated water ready in a martini glass or a highball tumbler as needed. A drop of food colouring could mark a special moment or a new name for the same drink. A wedge of lemon or umbrella could be tucked into boost the illusion. Everyone looked forward to those evenings so much. I just loved listening to the chatter of happy souls.

When the leader went off to deal with other matters. Jessica picked up her earlier conversation.

"The Study Leader said he has measurements of how connected people are to their stuff over time. Remember how important those things from their earlier lives were when they came in here?"

She continued, "A new scratch was a calamity. A breakage was cause to up meds or add new ones for depression. That still happens but he went through the stats to show that when people have a more active social life, more connections, they seem to need the physical stuff less. Do you find that?"

I shrugged a questionable nod. Maybe it was true. What I had wanted was the visual reminder of happy moments of my past. My pictures did that and the kids digitized them down to a thumb drive. So, my physical demands compressed to insignificance as long as I had a playback unit. It was the organ that I couldn't do without, and the keyboard that took up the room space after the organ went to the Dining Room here. That piece of stuff and the music that went with it, the physical pile of paper, had defined me. It was to me what the teacups were to the Store Lady, what the violin and cello were to the Mrs. Beresford. So, stuff matters. I guess it is a problem when you have so many things that you can't give the pieces value relative to each other - when everything is equally significant - or trivial. Then a loss of any is a lesion that won't heal.

I dug through my pockets to find my Post-it pad. All I got was a wrinkled previous note. On the back of it I scribbled, *Life simpler with less stuff. More fun with social stu...* and my pen ran out.

"I get it," Jess said. "By the way, a serious study of the before and after data raised a question. Did you guys fudge the scores somehow? The fact man compared his results with studies all over the place and asked that question as a result."

I just held up my hands in confusion.

"He said that if those results were intentionally skewed, it opened the door on a level of research nobody seems to have explored - that seniors might be capable of deceit and organization, aided by skills retained from earlier vocations.

Maybe I gave the follow up too much eyebrow elevation.

"*Busted*," I thought.

She smiled in return.

"In the meantime, I have another problem. I've got a Trustee meeting to attend and at it, my proposal to sell the violin is to be discussed. I can't think that will go well but at least I gave it a try.

I patted her on the shoulder and nodded encouragement.

"Thanks," she said.

26
THE FIDDLER

Mrs. Beresford actually seemed to be considering
Margaret's suggestion to sell the Strad and use the
proceeds to finance an on-going educational string
program. Having never expected to get past the proposal
stage, Jessica was rather unprepared when Mrs.
Beresford asked for details about the plan she had
imagined. It was obvious from the rest of that
conversation, that Mrs. Beresford was imagining some
sort of university string program that the Foundation
would be contributing to, as it sponsored classical
training for those worthy of aspiring to the classical

concert stage. Margaret didn't feel so limited. Thank God for Sam; Margaret's friend was a fiddler as well as an inventor.

By the time we got to the old Irish pub where Sam played, it was late. We had to park two blocks away and dodge through the thickening rain to the door. Pulling the door open, we pushed our way into a warm wall of sound within. The light was subdued, not dark. Gleaming glasses in racks hung beside dark trim and gilded signs. "*Superior Old Irish Whiskeys*," said one; "*Purveyors Of Fine Stouts and Ales*," said another. Surfaces were polished with care and scratched with long use.

The place was packed. Margaret had called ahead when the traffic tied us to the wet street, so we were expected. Male eyes of the barkeep over the crowd before him, nodded and flicked towards the back wall. Margaret wedged her way through the crowd to find the manager of the place defending two seats on the bench and an upturned chair on a small table in the corner.

We dropped into place with relief as the manager squeezed past. By the time we had struggle out of our wet coats he was back with full pints.

"Sláinte!" Margaret said as she clinked her glass against Jessica's, then mine.

Lucy, a server, swung sideways as she returned from another table, shouted an introduction and got out a pencil and pad. I pointed to fish and chips on the menu card and held up one finger; my escorts ordered chicken wings and a monster salad to share.

I love the warmth of places like this. You're swaddled in the sounds of happy people, jammed elbow to elbow. Everyone is so excited to find a community with similar feelings. If you came in glum, you couldn't remain so for long.

I looked around; kids were playing tic-tac-toe, filling colouring books or playing iPad games while their parents were laughing at the other end of their table. Everyone but three cell phone operators were leaning forward energetically, excitedly, to talk across the table. They were seniors and servants; not a suit amongst them. All ignored the two huge screens displaying a hockey game to a cornered few. This time and space were all that mattered to most here.

I was halfway down my mug when I heard the first whine of a violin tuning. The band had to be on the other side of the room in the corner by the front door. That fiddle would be Sam's. Immediately conversation tipped downward as the vocalist called a welcome and hit the downbeat. An electronic base and a guitar thumped into action - amped up, rhythmic. The vocalist burst momentarily through any conversational remnants. Before he finished the first verse, new jokes and stories had found a way through his words.

Sam came in on the second song.

The collective pulse took a skip when he sounded the chords to *Father Kelly's Reconciliation*. Clapping started to accompany the music before the bottom of the first page and was thunderous before it ended. Applause said how people felt about that tune. A momentary silence fell as mugs were siphoned then set down as the next reel began. Wet boots stomping on the board floor joined more clapping and buried the guitar and base. Only Sam's flying fingers sounded above the hoots and shouts. I think there was some dancing going on out of sight. The room's adrenalin level notched up.

I had to see what was happening. As I stood, Jessica dropped her knapsack on my chair to stake my claim. She'd defend the territory. Margaret slid off the bench and led the way through a crossover behind the bar then between jammed tables holding a hundred more on the other side of the room. The end of the set was coming. I recognized the introduction to *The Sloop John B*.

"We came on the sloop John B, my gra…nd father and me," sang the guy with the guitar, all back of his throat and nasal.

"The beauty of the untrained voice," I thought. Did anyone else care? Not a whit.

"…I feel so broke up, I just wanna go home," wailed the vocalist.

And then the sound exploded.

"So, hoist up the John B's sails. See how the main sail's set…"

Every voice in the place seemed to have joined in the chorus. I've played in the biggest organs in the world, but I never felt surround sound like this. Dancing over this mob of voices was the obligato of Sam's violin.

Before the vocalist came in for the second verse, the basses in the crowd had set up, "Do-Do, Do do do," that buried the bass guitar.

"The first mate he got drunk. He broke in the Captain's trunk…" sang the leader over the thunder below his notes and then we were at the chorus again.

"So, hoist up the John B's sails …"

New voices had joined in harmony. Some doing spontaneous obbligatos where the violin had been. Sam was just holding the melody line.

"I wanna go home, … (let me go home)," came the off-beat entry of tenors around the room. The place was throbbing.

"Back in a while," shouted the lead into the microphone through the unaccompanied repeat of the chorus by the crowd.

He set down his guitar and turned off his iPad on the music stand. On the floor, I could see a clipboard with titles written in bold black - to be read from standing height. *John B* stood out above a line halfway down the page. There were two more pages sticking out below the top one.

I looked at Sam's music stand; there was no music, just a cup holder taped on the post and in the holder was a half glass of ale.

I tapped Margaret on the shoulder and pointed at the empty music stand.

She smiled back and leaned to shout in my ear, "He doesn't need any. If he doesn't know it already, he makes it up."

That hit me like a mallet.

Here was a folk musician who would be playing for hours, perfectly in sync with the rest of the ensemble, from memory or making it up like a jazz fiddler. In doing so, he had people jumping for joy, literally dancing in the aisles.

"Wonder when that last happened at a concert of mine," I thought. *"Rieu!"* I thought. *"His audiences do that either between the concert rows when cued, or along the edges of the square spontaneously. He plays a Strad too."*

"So, what other place can you name?" I was thinking as I held out my hand in supplication to ask a question. Margaret understood.

"Well, his uncle taught him the string names, before he went to school, but he's never had formal training till he signed up at college recently. He plays with me in the orchestra to work on his reading skills.

So now he can read music a bit but not as fast as he has to play here so somewhere down the page he just looks away and lets his fingers fly. I wish mine were as nimble as his. Everything you see up there he learned by ear and by practice."

Sam had spotted his girlfriend and headed our way. I waited to be introduced but quickly figured I was a third wheel. I nodded that I was retreating. My fish and fries were at my place when I got to the table along with a fresh pint. Jess sat before the platters she and Margaret would share.

"He has to talk to his fan club," Margaret explained when she rejoined us a few minutes later.

When I finish a concert especially if I'm at the console way up in a church gallery, and I hit the final chord, I get this feeling of oneness with music that is almost spiritual, like I'm in tune with something cosmic.

I remembered one time, glancing down the stairs from a loft in England and wondering if when I got down there, would people still be there? I felt so transported to somewhere else during the concert that I would not have been surprised to step out onto a foreign world. That was the feeling at the edges of consciousness in this crowd that night.

"This isn't alcoholic. This is community," I thought. *"For a lifetime, I've been trying to teach people to listen to subtlety and meanings in harmony and intervals. Everyone in this pub already seems to know what those in churches don't. Should I feel elated or depressed?"* I wondered.

The encore was Sam's tour de force. The band had finished its final set. The audience was thanked. Guitars were back in their stands. Hands were reaching to turn off amplifiers, when the audience seemed to realize the band had stopped. There were a couple shouts of "NO!" from around the room. Others took up the cry. The shouts quickly morphed into foot-stomping unison clapping of, *Ex... Press. Ex...Press.*

I had found my way to the edge of the dance floor and was about to retreat when this crescendo stopped me. The other bandsmen looked up, seemingly puzzled. Sam stood in the dark upstage corner, back to the crowd, looking intently into his open violin case. In that moment, I could see he wasn't packing his fiddle. His fingers were flicking the strings, silently checking his tuning. The audience was now pounding tables with flat hands, to accompany the stomps and clapping.

Sam, still facing the back of the stage, took a step backwards as though he was about to set down his instrument, but instead his bow swung up and came down on the strings. Slowly and softly a discordant double-stopped sound came from far away through the silence that accompanied his movement. The audience burst into cheers and stopped in a heartbeat to hear the next discord that fell into the silence from far away.

It was magical to hear. The whole room seemed to be holding its breath waiting for that next chord. There it was - a little louder now. Sam had taken another step back but had still not turned around. On the third chord he turned slowly and that turn raised the volume slightly more. The room was absolutely riveted on that violin and the image of an approaching train that the sound conjured up. I expected the *Orange Blossom Express* to come right through the back curtain.

In seconds, the pace had picked up. The other performers had recovered their instruments and were joining in under cover of Sam and his fiddle. I think the piece went on for ten minutes. Broad slides, vibrato, and pizzicati decorated a spontaneous performance that would never be repeated again. The room was clapping and cheering, all red-faced and whooping with excitement until the final chords faded away. The crowd was on their feet and shouting and laughing. They had been played as skillfully as the instruments held on stage and they loved it.

Margaret told us later it was all an act; all the movements well-rehearsed - not the music though. They all knew the melody, but each had a turn to shine with their improvising and sometimes, like this night's, were better than others.

"Just never know," she added.

I know I was breathless when it ended. I was glad to sit down just to collect myself.

As we stepped out into the drizzle left from the rain.

Margaret said, "That's what I want Mrs. Beresford's fortune to finance, I want her to make more like Sam."

27
THE STUFF INFECTION

"I'm the one who's torn up about it," Jessica complained. "It was even my idea to sell it. What was I thinking? I've been playing it for months to get it back into condition and now I have to hand it over to perfect strangers."

"Well, you have your old violin still," countered Margaret.

Margaret had taken Jess's idea to the Trustees not expecting the thought to be considered.

But then it was and now the process had run full circle.

"It was fine until the Strad dropped into your lap," she continued trying to pour oil on these troubled waters.

"I think it is a case of keeping the girl down on the farm after she's been to Paris," moaned Jessica

"What would you give to get it back?"

"I doubt I could ever reach the skill level to earn the money to buy it back or be in the run in a competition - well unless I became obsessive enough to never do anything else. It doesn't come easy so to make up for the small talent I do have, I have to work so much more just to do what those guys do without thinking. Sorry, I think there might to be more to life than a violin. I'd sooner do what Sam does."

"As though he doesn't work overtime to do that."

"I'm happy to be part of the orchestra - one of the many."

"So, the violin is off to tour the world again?"

"Yeah, we had to pass it over at the lawyers. I wondered if the guy who picked it up came in an armoured truck like the ones that service banks. It was all very formal and underwhelming. When all the boxes were checked off, he snapped down the lid, picked it up, shook hands around and left. It was so anticlimactic, but I felt I had just lost a friend. I should write a book about a violin travelling through time into the hands of a spoiled debutante, being banished to a closet because of her whim, and then being resurrected."

"I'll bet Hollywood would beat a path to your door," Margaret quipped but when it got no response she added, "we've got a gig at the end of the month, a wedding. I presume you'll be up for it?"

"I'll recover. Reminds me of that song from R & H - *South Pacific* I think. *'This nearly was mine,'* I think it goes."

"Not really. It was yours for a while. You just wanted to use someone else's stuff and not pay for it. Mind you, you cared for it like a loving parent, but can you really tell the difference in the sound?"

"Yeah I can," she said with a sigh. "It was more mellow, had a complexity that my own violin doesn't. Maybe it's in the overtones or the feel. Kind of hard to explain." She shook herself, "But now we're back to the real world and we'll go and play for the newlyweds. Do you think Sam might come and do some step dance stuff?"

"We're on for dinner, only. I think they got a DJ for later"

"Makes me laugh to think of Sam doing a jig and people getting food down their fronts."

*

"How does anyone have that much money to buy a violin?" Jessica asked as she held up the news item of the auction on her iPad at dinner that night. "It seems almost obscene to have that much income to …"

She found herself sputtering but lurched on.

"How much stuff does a person like that have when they can come up with that kind of cash with the wave of a card? I mean how big a closet would you have?"

She was plainly flabbergasted at the price paid for the violin.

"Well how big a closet did Mrs. Beresford store it in? Like maybe the size of a refrigerator?" Brad said. "Any idea how much the investment of that sort of cash will bring for the string program?"

"Mrs. Beresford told Margaret they can count on three million annually but that is allowing a small excess to accumulate - slush money, I think it would be called. I didn't believe her when she said what it sold for. I had to callus the news report myself," Jessica replied.

"And now the hard part begins," Brad said. "How does the committee find people worthy of the gift?"

"Those are dangerous words, sir," Jessica snapped. "When you say *worthy*, it implies you meet some standard. Who decides the standard? And *gift* could be considered condescending."

Brad quickly buried his nose in his coffee cup looking for the dregs.

He recalled that Jessica was concluding an Arts and Ethics course this semester.

"Margaret suggested Sam be paid to travel and seek fiddler prospects this summer. He refused to give up his gig with the band, but the tour idea is getting traction. They all go together. He has a network of folk fiddlers around the country that he could tap for aspiring kids they might know."

"I understand the cello is back from the shop and Margaret is tasked with playing it back into shape," Brad added.

Jessica burst back in with a little heat - but still with a smile.

"Serves her right," Jessica said. "She wondered why I missed the violin so much. It's her turn to get what she dished out. Give her six months and she'll be sleeping with the thing!"

I reached over to pat her hand.

"You sound a bit out of sorts," Brad added.

Jessica looked down and went tight-lipped.

"I am. I really am," she said heatedly.

She drew a deep breath to steady herself and was blinking furiously.

"I think the Teacup lady must have died."

We both nodded. The hearse had arrived after lunch while Jessica was at school. I think she said she had an exam.

"I passed a cleaning cart on my way here for dinner. There was one of those translucent plastic bags on it. It was tied up, but I could see it had clothes in it and all those teacups she so treasured."

She continued, "All her stuff is going in the garbage. All those pretty things she was so happy to tell you about. Everyone knew she made it up, but it made her light up when you asked about them. And as soon as she's out of sight … It really is rude!"

"It's stuff," Brad said.

Jessica jumped up from the table and bolted for the door.

"It's just stuff," Brad repeated.

I found out from Eva at bedtime that Jessica had arrived like a thundercloud at the Receiving Area and climbed into the dumpster to find the bag. She came back with Margaret and they carried the china cabinet from Mrs. Pekot's room back from the Loading Dock to their own room also.

With a day of studying for her next exam, Jessica joined us for coffee in mid-morning.

She pushed a utility cart from the kitchen with Mrs. Pekot's teacups proudly displayed. I looked at Brad. I nodded a chin to him. He had to explain.

We took our tea in the decorative cups. Jessica explained how every sip was a statement against treating people like garbage. She wondered why everyone else was steered to the institutional mugs on the other cart.

Brad had to explain that management wouldn't, indeed couldn't, let her put them out unless they were properly washed.

Jessica was stunned.

"We can't use these beautiful cups and saucers in memory of a fine woman and friend of us all?" she burst out.

We had to admit that this spread of elegance trumped the institutional mug line up, opposite.

"This is an institute regulated by health rules about dishes. They have to go through the sterilizing cycle on the washing machine which will take all the decorative gilding off, or you have to wash them by hand in a two sink process with soap in one and disinfectant in the other. Sorry but their license is on the line if they don't adhere to the regs."

As Jessica looked at her beautiful Royal Worcester cup, Brad threw out the lifeline.

"But we can share tea in them privately, in our rooms or wherever. We just steal the pot and bring it back later."

"Doesn't anyone complain?" she asked.

"When breakfast is being cleared up, it is easy to steal an empty pot then and when the fresh ones come out at teatime, we just substitute," Brad confessed.

"It's easiest if we use my walker to do the transfer. You can stuff it in a bag in the carrier basket. Otherwise you have to ask for tea to be served officially in your room. They want to know why. A staff member has to pour it so that nobody gets burned. We do it our way as long as we can get away with it."

"So," Brad stood, "shall we take our tea to your place or mine?"

"Haven't had an offer like that in a long time," Jessica replied. "Come to my place. Marg's cookies are there, and you'll probably get more to brag about if you said you got the invite by one of the students to drop over. Make me a scandal though and you'll never see another of those cookies again."

"Got it."

Brad set his cup on Jessica's trolley and let her lead the way.

He scooped up the tea carafe from the other trolley and hid it in his carrier before following.

The girls had a suite meant for married couples. It had a central room with two bedrooms or a bedroom and office leading off from it; there was the standard short hallway with a bathroom on one side, and dressing or storage on the other. The central space could be a sitting area, kitchen area and dining space for two. The girls had managed to get a small proper stove to go with the microwave oven hung below the over-counter cupboards and above the sub-counter refrigerator. It had no dishwasher. Had it been for seniors it would only have had a bar fridge and microwave to go with the single well sink.

Mrs. Pekot's china cabinet held center stage in the room. Light from the nearby window shone through the glass sides and sparkled on the glass shelving and teacups. The top shelf held the teacups Jessica had saved.

On top of the cabinet, above eye level and just peeking around the ornate top moulding, I could see a blue-coloured plush bag with a gold tassel about the neck. I knew what was in it.

"Some of the cups broke," Jessica said pointing to the four saucers stacked in the corner of the shelf as she replaced the ones that had been on the cart, for others to use, in the cabinet.

I noticed she stacked the saucers four high and nested the cups sideways on them the way they had been in my house. The crowded collection was not as attractively displayed because of the clutter below. As she closed the glass-paneled doors, she continued.

"I never realized when we were in your house how hard it must have been for you to get rid of all those things your wife had. I must confess, I went to the dealer who took them and bought these four back."

She pointed to the stack in the back corner on top of the saucers from the broken cups.

"So, my experience at your house was sensitivity training for me. I understand how meaningful things like that can be. I love the care and pride that cups like this represent in a person's life; if those cups and the candelabra are representatives of your wife's taste and style, I wish I had met her."

That made my breath catch in my throat. I tried to mouth a "Thank-you" and sat down. *Welcome to stuff,* I wrote on a Post-it and passed it across then returned to my tea. The dregs were cold. Brad noticed and pulled the hot pot from his carrier.

Brad followed my gaze after pouring my tea and added, "I like what you've done with rest of the space."

It was a joking comment about the jumble of music scores, texts, magazines, and revues that filled it.

"It represents the disordered mind of its previous owner. Should I tell you how long it has taken me to place each piece in precisely that arrangement?" Jessica explained with a straight face. "And if you notice its clutter changes with time, it is yet another statement of the dynamic nature of mindfulness."

She was having fun with Brad as to who would get the last word.

"Would you say that again?" Brad asked. "I want to print it on a card and hang it on the wall in my room to drive off the obsessive cleaners we have here." He was not expecting to be caught out.

Jessica handed him a pencil and a piece of paper from the dining table.

"It represents the disordered … am I going too fast?"

Tossing down the pencil in mock frustration Brad said, "I'll call you to deliver the speech, when I need it."

I think he was actually a little pleased at her comeback.

Summer Jobs? I wrote on my next Post-it.

"Margaret is travelling with the band as technical support and to set up the meetings with prospects for the string program. When she's got some actual candidates, she can figure out the next steps, so that is what she's doing. Between playing the Strad back into shape and that contract she'll be able to pay her way next semester. I'm working in the Library again. We got a big collection of personal stuff donated to the University and it has to be catalogued. After working on your material last year, I was the strongest candidate in the competition for the job so I can live here and do that. Old stuff is becoming my job."

"I hadn't thought of stuff as a source of employment, but I guess it is if you count the recyclers and the antique dealers - and the archivists of course," I thought.

Start? I scribbled.

"Well, my last exam was yesterday. I can take off a couple weeks though we have some June weddings to get music up for but I'm going to be a taking it easy for a while. The library job is also a nine-to-five, so I have my nights free … and Stat holidays. How good is that? I might even find a social life?"

28
BACK TO TEACHING

Sunday after lunch, I was writing my notes in my
performance journal when Jessica knocked at the door.

"Do you have time to chat?" she asked.

I smiled and pointed to her then my mouth. Then I
cupped my ear to say I would listen.

She laughed and stepped in as I held the door open.

"Is that your journal?" she asked as she proceeded
me into my bachelor pad as I think about it.

I nodded.

"I heard about this. May I look at it?"

I nodded again and went to retrieve the chair from my dressing room for her to sit on. I sat on the bench for my keyboard.

"You are brutally frank and detailed. You even mention pages and phrases to fix."

I held up a finger to my lips to suggest it was secret.

She laughed and looked back at a few more pages.

"When did you start doing this?"

I showed my height when I started.

"Your whole life? What do you do when the book is full?"

I pointed to the drawers of the filing cabinet below.

"May I?"

I nodded and she pulled open the top one then the next.

"Every drawer is full?" She was incredulous.

I nodded. *Close enough,* I thought.

She slid the drawer closed and took the empty seat.

"Will you divide the collection between your children or does one get them all, when you're gone?"

I shook my head. *My children live lives that don't include this stuff,* I acknowledged to myself.

I caught the flicker of surprise she showed followed by the sag of sadness as she realized where all these tomes would go.

She'd been part of the process of disposing of piles of paper in my house only a year or so before. Her eyes dropped to her lap but when they came up, I think they were those of the woman who rescued the bag from the dumpster.

"I got off track," she said. "I really came in to ask if you teach still? I have a whole summer here in town, but I wondered if I could take keyboard lessons from you? You know I play the violin, but I just wanted to broaden my skills and I thought if you were interested, I'd ask. I can pay the going rate." The last words tumbled out in a rush.

I raised my eyebrows and searched around for my pencil and Post-its.

Start? I wrote.

"Whenever you are available."

I moved off the bench and pointed to it.

"Now?" she asked genuinely surprised.

I stood to surrender the bench at the keyboard. My large screen monitor was on the music stand. I called up a search and typed in a title.

She looked at the music in surprise; I waved her forward.

She was uncertain where to put her hands. She wasn't an absolute novice. She'd been around music long enough to have a speaking acquaintance with a keyboard, if only to tune her violin, but it seemed the last act of reluctance before she jumped off the cliff. I pointed to the treble clef and moved her right thumb to middle C. I stretched her hand so her fourth finger played the G so fifth could play the A then waved her forward. She knew note value. I tapped the frame slowly for the tempo and she pecked out the most famous tune in any string player's education - the Suzuki international anthem.

Thank you, Herr Mozart.

I picked up the tempo. She followed quickly. I came to her left side and illustrated how to play the root then inverted chords to accompany the melody line in the right. That took a little longer to master.

I then shifted her over and played several improvs on the right while she repeated the bass chords, signing she could make any she wanted. She smiled and started to experiment when I was out of the way. After doodling for a while, I handed her a note.

Next week, same time, 3 improvs & chording.

She smiled then reached for her purse.

I held up fingers in an 'X'.

She protested.

I gave her a no-nonsense glare over my glasses. As she slid off the bench, I pulled the bottom drawer of the filing cabinet open. My next journal lay there ready when the current one was full. I had months of pages left in the one I was using. I pulled out the new one and handed it to her.

Again, she protested and got 'The Glare' amped up.

I opened mine to show her the headings she needed to put in her book and gave her the pen to do it. I shooed her out before she could fill them in indicating I wanted a nap. With a big sigh and a happy heart, I dozed off wondering what to do at her next lesson.

*

"How will you pick them?" I texted on my new smart phone.

"Aren't you getting progressive," Margaret said when she answered the unexpected message while we had tea in her suite, on Jessica's cups.

I guess I hadn't texted her before. Kids always seem surprised when seniors learn things; they spend so long not learning life's current necessities; they don't seem to acknowledge that we all spent a lifetime without the trivia they think are necessities, just as they disdain most of what we prize. Jessica was at work.

While she poured, I'd been tapping away. I guess she thought I was playing some game.

I've noticed many young people monkey with their phones even while sitting with others. Maybe it's a new norm. Anyway, it was the best I could do in the moment. It still felt silly to type in a message, send it God Knows Where, to contact the person standing beside me. I'd forgotten my iPad back in my room, I think. Maybe it's on the organ.

I waved her on. Brad reached for another cookie.

"Well, Sam and I made a list of people they met on their tour. There are probably forty. Sam says they all have skills appropriate to their level. I mean some are just starting out and others have been fiddlers for years. All are trying to juggle jobs or school or families or all of the above. All would like to get better but are stalled for various reasons. She's got to prepare a list of criteria for the selection process and honestly, it is my worst nightmare."

"But out of your sleeplessness, something tells me you've got some thoughts," Brad interjected.

"Well I think someone really needs to want to do it - like almost obsessively - no there is *no almost* about it. I think they have to have fun, like they do that instead of watching TV or playing a game, so oddly, they may seem rather anti-social."

She paused, "I really think they should be curious or creative in what they do with the instrument - try new things. Like it or not, I think they have to have a way to write whatever they're doing, down. It doesn't have to be on paper, but they need to have what I call the Joplin factor."

She continued, "Jessica told me about you teaching her keyboard while we were away. She shared your history lesson about how musicians need to leave a trail of notational crumbs - the new stuff by which we communicate. You have made the case for notation. A recording won't do."

I had only introduced Jessica to Joplin and ragtime recently, as part of her developing keyboard playing.

"The only reason Joplin's work survived was because he wrote it down. There were many honky-tonk piano players in that day, but we don't know what they did because they were illiterate."

"Didn't stop the music or entertainment, just the ability to pass it along. Passing it along was a feature that Mrs. Beresford and the Trust held dear, and legacies have to be in a form that will travel through time".

I had to hold my tongue on that; I am a believer in the power of paper. Paper records survived centuries - longer than the headstone of the people who made them - until the mass of those collections got to what I had in my house. Now all that is on a gadget the size of my finger. And it is available as long as the lights stay on. But you'll never convince me that paper isn't the long-term solution to music.

"And how will you determine each candidate's strength in these qualities? Do people get a scorecard?" asked Brad. "Consensus would be good, I guess. So, you better write down the rules, the policy."

"That is where I want to scream," Margaret confessed.

"How do you separate one excellent candidate from another? The legacy of all that drives me to late nights. Why is it so hard to do something good?" Margaret groaned.

"Work on making cookies instead," suggested Brad. "They are always good. Every time you make another batch you are resurrecting an experience from the past and putting the individual stamp on it. Commercial will never approach what you have learned to do. I think there is that objective at Cookie Central - the perfect cookie - but in order to bake a billion of them and achieve world domination over something, they give up the personal touch, the slightly more ginger or molasses, the half-minute less in the oven, the essence of the coffee beside the cooling cookies that was trapped in the dough. Robotic cookies for cookie-cut people."

"Aren't you getting philosophical," Margaret said.

"All I want to do is spread around the money to educate a bunch of violin and fiddle players and there are too many."

"Have you thought to ask the players?" I wrote.

"Pardon? Are you suggesting another criteria might be awareness what they think they need?" Margaret asked. "I like that."

"Could the players listen and talk to each other and vote on a ranked ballot, who should get whatever from among their midst?" Brad asked.

"Wouldn't they each vote for themselves?"

"Do you think they wonder how to advance their field? Might they be able to spot best, what others need? Do they each need the same kind of support? Don't you think they would share?"

"Emma H. Ask her about altruism studies." I pecked into my telephone and sent it.

"Who is this?" asked Jessica. She showed the name to Brad.

"You're letting a cat out of the bag here, buddy," he cautioned and looked at me with a bit of a scowl.

Brad turned back to Margaret and said, "She knows a lot about studies of people who were given choices to be selfish or generous to others. We'd be obliged if you kept her secret as a source. But if you explained your task, I'm sure she could design a program that would both work for the trust and give you documentation that would support its continuation. You might even get a Master's Thesis out of it if you want one. She lives down the hall two rooms past Mrs. Beresford."

I stood to leave. Empty cup; empty pot; empty cookie plate; time to go. The teacup display was right at eye level. Margaret caught me looking at her roommate's display. I put a hand over my heart and smiled back at her. She seemed aware that she'd caught me in an emotional moment and gave me a big hug.

"How can she ever appreciate what a display like that meant in our young married life?" I thought. *"If a picture was worth a thousand words, those teacups were worth ten thousand pictures in what they said about a society that had vanished except for relics like me. Such stuff were the medals of service and remembrance and even one-up-womanship. They were the token symbols of lineages and relations not one university graduate in a hundred could personally duplicate. And Jessica had rescued them from a dumpster. Good on her! Will she ever realize the significance of her sentimental reaction? Will the 'wow' from that moment drive her into compulsive collection - a stuff collector?"*

I broke the hug and stepped back. We shared a wistful smile as Brad tugged my sleeve. He'd opened the door and was waiting for me.

*

"Emma is some woman," Jessica said. "Margaret can't say enough about her. She designed a process by which every person on their list sends in their rendition of two named pieces, and a personal composition. No more than ten minutes total for all three. That is how they get to go to the next stage. If they don't submit, they're out."

She handed over a blank application form. We would get to her lesson later.

"Once they get the pieces," she said, "Emma will number them and then bundle them in packages randomly."

She continued, "Each person has to listen to, and evaluate, a total of twenty pieces but they have no idea whose they are and the player of one piece might not be the one who plays the one after, so it really is a blind study. Part of the evaluation is to suggest skills the player should work on." She passed a blank evaluation form.

"If they do that, then they can send in their evaluations with a statement of what they think they need in order to progress - five hundred word maximum - and ranking of their own needs relative to those they listened to. One woman said she just needs someone to make meals for the family to give her two hours a day to practice. Another kid said he needs less homework. She never expected anything like that. What really shocked her to her socks was that nearly everyone wanted to step back and let others get the funding or training ahead of them."

I nodded and returned the paper. It sounded like a good plan; I was not surprised at the results.

"The plan is to offer appropriate support to about twenty, maybe twenty-five and compare them with a similar number being offered support in a standard classical music program at university. Can you see the cross-referencing and insight something like this could develop?" She was really getting excited.

I let her go on a bit before I pointed to the music stand and tapped my watch.

"Got it, but I didn't do much for you this week."

*

Mrs. Beresford took over Brad's place at my table when he died just after Thanksgiving.

"I think I'll move out," he had said only the night before at dinner and then next morning he was gone.

I had thought it was more hyperbole arising from the fact that it was his turn to read to the children who would be coming in later in the week. *"God, I miss him,"* I thought. His wry observation of life was something I'd grown used to.

It was Eva who brought his ebony statue to me at coffee time that morning.

"He's made all the arrangements," she said. "He had no children. He told me any money he had was in some insurance thing that would pay to people or charities when they showed up with his death certificate. I don't know if he has an executor or if the Public Whoever has to look after his final affairs. There sure is little enough to dispose of. I think his whole wardrobe would fit into a big suitcase. He has a dresser from Ikea - and then there is this." She set down the carving in the chair opposite me.

I guess I knew it would happen soon but thought back on the months I chose not to dwell on the prospect.

More unmade decisions. Since summer he'd added oxygen to his walker. I wondered if he could have overdosed on some of his meds but wasn't going to say anything - like I could anyway? *"Very funny, Scottman."*

I was in the depths of that thought and had to struggle up the other side when I realized that the Business Administrator had appeared in front of me. She did have a talent for timing.

"We're all sorry Mr. Daniels is gone. I know you had become good friends. He delivered an envelope to me two weeks ago with instructions to open it if he died. Inside it was this letter."

She handed across a padded envelope.

It took me a moment to realize she was talking about Brad. I couldn't recall the last time I'd used his surname.

"Sorry to impose on you one last time," the letter began.

I set it down and just looked up at the ceiling and took a couple deep breaths. The administrator just put a hand on my arm. Thank goodness she didn't ask if I was alright. Tilted back in the chair opposite, Jonas, the statue, studied the ceiling, avoiding eye contact.

I'd been named executor. This was his Will - signed, dated, witnessed. Another sheet was a list of institutions to contact. Numbers for Social Insurance, Health, Driver's License Bank Account. His Passport came out with the bunch of cards.

"*A final tax return is needed,*" the letter continued "*to take care of any leftover stuff.*" A name and address of an accountant and bank followed. "*Ask Mrs. Beresford's lawyer. He'll tell you no probate is needed. I'm worth less than five thousand. Give whatever is in my bank account to the Male Voice Choir for a night or two at the bar. Maybe they'll take Jonas as their mascot.*"

"My ashes will come back to you in a plastic bag inside a cardboard box. One of Bach's cantatas was probably pulped in the making of that box. Nice to have such company. Sprinkle me in the garden after dark and recycle the bag and box, please."

There was a pencil addition to the typing. *"You have been a good friend, but you can't sing worth a damn. See you sometime … maybe."*

The Business Administrator saw how the air went out of my balloon when I got to the bottom of the page. She did the most tender thing.

She touched my arm and said, "We'll help you do all the formalities."

I remember how liberating that statement was. And she was as good as her word. Brad is now laid to rest and so can I - well except for Jonas and the other thing.

So those are the thoughts that come back as my new table-mate approaches. I could tell just by her step how anxious she was to update me on the Proceedings of the Strad Program. I don't think she drew a silent breath until she had finished telling me what an asset to decision-making she found Margaret to be, the effect of the recent stock market changes on the portfolio and how it might affect the number they could enroll next year.

Before she could relate the individual progress of all fifty musicians in the program, I waved my hands in the "T" sign for a time-out. She didn't recognize the sign.

"What?" she asked as though she was surprised to be interrupted.

It's not her fault. She is lonely. Few people want to talk to her around here, I've observed. I don't know if I've ever heard her ask a question. In her world everyone stopped to listen to what she had said. I guess it's part of the behavioural stuff she collected along the way.

Anyway, when I held up my hands, it was one of the passing kitchen staff who was collecting plates, translated.

"Oh," she said with surprise. "I didn't know that."

I took the last sip of my tea.

"You asked me to play the last chord of a fugue you were practicing a while ago. Could we try that again?"

I led the way and handed her earphones once I'd opened the organ. It is not a long piece. When I got to the last page, she followed me down and positioned her hands again as she had done before. I could sense her getting ready during the ritard to the final bar. This time she came in bang on tempo and with the major chord written. I guess that was as good an apology as I would get. It said done.

"There," she proclaimed.

I nodded and gave her a thumbs up, but she was already moving away.

I sat, before bed, looking at all the faces on the banner my children had created, as I had so often before. Jonas has joined me now. The Choir didn't want to drag him around, though they gladly toasted Brad long and often with what he contributed to their party fund. I agreed that the statue would have been badly beaten up being trotted all over the place like some garden gnome. And it was heavy enough to require an athletic and fit carrier - not so easy to find amongst a bunch of senior singers. So, Jonas keeps watch with the other silent figures, on my room and over me in the darkness. He is also the guardian of what's left of Brad's books.

There were two books to start. Brad never showed them to me, but it was as much a journal as he ever kept, I guess.

When he walked out of his apartment, he said he was just walking away from all that stuff. Well, not quite. He said that his suitcases contained that season's clothes in one and off-season stuff in the other. I guess I had presumed he meant off-season clothes. In the other case I found two of the biggest three-ring binders that suppliers sell.

The binders contained plastic pages, heat-sealed into pockets that might have held photographs in a by-gone day. Each pocket contained two beer or drink coasters, one facing each way. Each was dated and the place where he had enjoyed the drink was named on the back - invisible until you took it out of the sleeve. On a few were what I presumed were the names of friends at the table. There was not one woman's name.

The collection spanned forty years, chronologically arranged. I didn't count them all but there were hundreds of tokens to memories that were his. He never shared them with anyone I knew. Restaurants and pubs and hotels around the world were noted.

The ones with people's names on, I've separated out.
They will stay in my room under Jonas's watchful gaze.
The others are moving onto the tables on Pub night or
when the choir is sharing our space. Already, they have
spawned chat amongst those who remember that city, or
even hotel. I'm sure Brad would be happy to hear the
memories that his items have jogged. From those tables,
the coasters move to the recycle bin. So, his pile of stuff
shrinks.

I think of how my own stuff has shrunk since my stroke.
I'm only a memory to a few now; my life is stored in a
device the size of a keyboard key. It seems appropriate.
Hiram Weaver said I'd wonder why I didn't downsize
sooner. I never wondered that. I know why I didn't.
Until my kids came up with the digitizing scheme, all
that paper was as much me as the organ I played on. But
even as I stare at that display screen, I regret that I don't
have the paper to hand on. Paper has stood the test of
time; that thought still keeps coming back to me. That
memory stick stuck in the back of a computer is a fad

that will pass as fast as I will. If nobody updates it, all that I was, just becomes … unreadable.

The streetlight that shows through my window lights up my Banner of Memorable People. A single sliver of light makes it across to Mr. Bach and the collage of the Halls of Great Organs. If I died, the banner would roll up in a mailing tube Maybe it would make a bunch of pillow covers. Would anyone lounging on them know on whose shoulders they lay? I wonder if the pictures would come out of their frames or just be tossed in the dumpster as is? Maybe Jessica would rescue them. That might be a sign that my virus had infected her. There is something mischievous about sending the Stuff Syndrome across another generation.

I thought of Brad's ashes in the garden beyond my window - invisible to all but I who had sprinkled them there. With them gone, he will only last as long as I do, I guess, except in some database.

He didn't do anything world famous, so he is stuff only to those who knew him. When they go … Does it really count, being knowable only to an algorithm? Only tangible relics bring any awareness of our existence. Someone curious might want to know where Jonas or the coasters came from or what significance gave them meaning. But without the context, what difference?

So I drift off to sleep aware that the stuff I got so used to and which ensnared me for so long, is only material on loan … for me to manipulate for a while before it and I become atomized stuff in a digital world, a memory to others or a recycled thing like Bach and the box of Brad's ashes.

ADDITIONAL TITLES FROM THIS AUTHOR

DUTY'S DAD
DUTY'S SON
DUTY'S DAUGHTER
ACTS OF REMEMBRANCE

WWW.PANDAMONIUMPUBLISHING.COM

www.ingramcontent.com/pod-product-compliance
Lightning Source LLC
Chambersburg PA
CBHW050916030726
47503CB00007BB/2327